KU-039-587

THE WORST KIND OF WANT

LISKA JACOBS

HODDER

First published in the USA in 2019 by MCD
An imprint of Farrar, Strauss and Giroux

First published in Great Britain in 2020 by Hodder & Stoughton
An Hachette UK company

This paperback edition published in 2020

1

Copyright © Liska Jacobs 2019

The right of Liska Jacobs to be identified as the Author of the Work
has been asserted by her in accordance with the Copyright,
Designs and Patents Act 1988.

Designed by Abby Kagan

All rights reserved. No part of this publication may be reproduced, stored in a
retrieval system, or transmitted, in any form or by any means without the prior
written permission of the publisher, nor be otherwise circulated in any form of
binding or cover other than that in which it is published and without a similar
condition being imposed on the subsequent purchaser.

All characters in this publication are fictitious and any resemblance
to real persons, living or dead, is purely coincidental.

A CIP catalogue record for this title is available from the British Library

Paperback ISBN 978 1 529 33406 7
eBook ISBN 978 1 529 33407 4

Typeset in Adobe Caslon Pro

Printed and bound in Great Britain by Clays Ltd, Elcograf S.p.A.

Hodder & Stoughton policy is to use papers that are natural,
renewable and recyclable products and made from wood grown in sustainable
forests. The logging and manufacturing processes are expected to conform
to the environmental regulations of the country of origin.

Hodder & Stoughton Ltd
Carmelite House
50 Victoria Embankment
London EC4Y 0DZ

www.hodder.co.uk

FOR MY SIBLINGS,

Ariel, Rachel, and Willy

Nothing at all in the world can perish, you have to believe me; things merely vary and change their appearance.

—*Metamorphoses*, Ovid

THE WORST KIND
OF WANT

My first thought when I overhear them is that no one would mistake Emily for being the same age as our mother.

"Pricilla is her *daughter*," the petite Filipino orderly is saying.

I had been looking for the social worker and paused just outside the door. They're folding laundry, the welcome smell of the commercial fabric softener overpowering the other, ranker, smells of the nursing home—urine, dust, sterilizer, probably mold.

"Are you sure she's not Mrs. Messing's sister?"

I feel the question like a pinprick, not on the surface of my skin, but from the inside, where my soft organs live. I imagine the orderly nodding, because of course she's sure. I am only forty-three.

"I *think* so."

When I return to my mom's room, it's like seeing it for the first time: there on the bedside table are my notes, lists of medications, doctors' phone numbers. Next to the trash can is a scattered pile of orange peels. A pale blue curtain used to divide the room is pushed back, revealing a wheelchair in the corner. I can hear the oxygen concentrator on the other side of her bed, pumping air into the tube beneath her nose. There is a huge vase of roses and hoary stock, sent from Guy, their colors bright against the drab, and on the muted TV, Fox News or CNN—it doesn't matter. She just likes the company.

"Mom." My voice cracks. "You shouldn't make a mess, the nurses have enough to do." I collect the orange rinds without looking at her and put them in the trash.

"I'm so uncomfortable," she complains. "And I don't like the nurse on duty tonight. She's the one I told you about. Big Russian woman." She motions with her arms, nearly catching the oxygen tube with her wedding ring. "She's always bossing me around. She made me eat fish last night. *Tilapia*. It was so gross, Pricilla. You can't imagine. You know what you can do? Go to Chick-fil-A and get me a sandwich. See if you can sneak in some gin, what does it matter! I'm dying anyways."

I struggle with the window. "For the hundredth time, you aren't dying. You're rehabilitating."

"Why do you want the window open? It's ninety degrees out."

The frame gives and a gust of warm air floods the room. I close my eyes and imagine the green parrots that flock to the palms and jacarandas before sunset, and the color of the sky over the Pacific—pinks and oranges and fog rolling in. I try to picture something beautiful, anything other than this ammonia-mopped room where I have spent the last two weeks. The chemical fumes stinging my eyes, drying out my mouth. I can feel it eating away at the lining of my nostrils.

My mother is waiting for a response. I can sense her annoyance. Mrs. Louise Messing does not like to be kept waiting, she does not like to feel ignored. But I need one more moment, just one. There are bars on the condo windows across the street. I close my eyes. The relentless pumping and whirring of her various machinery, the beeping coming from somewhere down the hall. I try to steady my breathing.

"Why can't I come home?" Her voice is sharp now. "What's the use of having a daughter live with you if she can't take care of you when you need it?"

I turn back to her. She's gesturing to the wallpaper peeling in the corner of the room and making a face. "You've dumped me in a real shit hole."

"You didn't mind it when Dad was here." I try not to study her face, but I can't help it. That etched delicate skin, the loose bit that hangs below the jaw. The orderlies' comments replay in a loop. I swallow.

"Remember how you liked to have lunch with Dad in the courtyard? Do you want me to see if we can arrange that? It's hot today, but tomorrow's supposed to be nice."

My mom purses her thin lips, clears something ugly and wet-sounding from her throat. "Do *you* remember that he died here?"

I'm not doing a good job of pacifying her. But I'm tired, the continuous buzz of the nursing home is wearing me down; the ammonia is making me dizzy. The room feels too small for my mother, and me, and all this equipment.

"That was a long time ago." I sigh. "Places age too." I start to put my notes away.

Her façade slips then. "You're not leaving? I thought you'd stay for dinner. You need to tell the staff I want spaghetti *with sauce*—last week it was only noodles and meatballs. They'll listen to you."

"I'm staying for dinner, like always."

We're quiet for a moment. I can tell she feels vulnerable now. She pretends to be preoccupied with the lace on her robe. She needs me to stay, to be here with her. There is a repetitive ringing at the nurses' station, as if someone somewhere in the facility is pressing a button for help and being ignored. I want—no, I *need* to get out of here.

"Did I tell you that Paul called?" I ask, trying to sound casual.

Her face lights up and for a moment I can see that old beauty. The sharp cheekbones; the expressive blue-gray eyes, once described as "glittering" in a review by the *Times*.

"Are they coming to visit? Did you talk to Hannah? Oh, I wish he hadn't taken my *only* granddaughter to Italy. I haven't seen her since, since—" She lets out a tragic moan. "Your poor sister."

She won't talk to me, my brother-in-law had said about my niece. He had called from their apartment in Rome, I could hear the faint wail of foreign sirens, of church bells. *She's got none of your coolheadedness, your reasonableness.* I thought he might list every "-ness". *Cilla is: politeness, calmness, fastidiousness.* Instead he rattled on about deadlines for the book he was writing with his colleague. How Hannah needed someone to watch out for her, how she was getting into all sorts of trouble. Caught smoking, ditching her Italian class—the last straw had involved the carabinieri. The police had picked her up for stealing nail polish from a department store. Paul was forced to pay an exorbitant fine. *Cilla, please. You will come, won't you? I'm at my wits' end.* Just hearing his voice made me think of Hannah, years ago, a chunky baby, nearly bald except for some fine blond frizz. Paul laughing at how her face scrunched up after sucking on a lemon slice, stolen from my sister's drink. *You don't want to eat that, my love*—Emily's voice, clear and bright, ringing out across the distance.

"Hannah is acting out. She's in trouble." I'm careful with

how to word this next part, my mom watching me. "He asked if I would come for the rest of the summer."

Those steely eyes go wide. "And what did you say? Did you tell him I'm in a nursing home and need you here?"

"Almost exactly that," I assure her, which is true. Only now the breeze coming from the window is blowing back the curtain, and I think I can smell the mock orange along the freeway overpasses, the honeysuckle bursting over fences and walls. What I mean is, I have an overwhelming desire to flee.

Mom gestures to the corner of the room, believing the conversation over. "Did you know they're rounded like that so it's easier to clean? Can you imagine? The urine and feces and whatever else, *ick*."

"Hannah is fifteen," I continue. "Do you remember what Emily and I were like at that age?"

"You were fine." She smiles. "But Emily." She looks away.

I press harder: "And Paul says Hannah is taking after her."

"Well, she can come keep you company. The house is too big for you to be on your own."

"She can't. She's in an accelerated Italian program, and they already have plans to summer in Puglia with friends. It would kill Hannah not to go." I pause, trying hard not to sound desperate. "The doctor and nurses will take excellent care of you while I'm gone. I'll make sure of it."

I try to kiss her cheek, but she turns and I end up kissing the top of her head.

"So, you're going to leave me here alone."

"Guy can visit every few days."

"With that girlfriend, what is she, twenty-three? He should have married you. I still don't know how you messed *that* up."

I try not to flinch. "I'll call and e-mail. We could FaceTime on your iPad."

"You're dead set on leaving," she says, eyes narrowed. But then, ever the actress, they fill just as quickly with tears. "I wish I could go with you. Your dad and I spent a whole summer in Europe before you girls were born."

"I'll bring you back something nice."

"I should hope so—oh, I forgot. Did you find the social worker? I can't remember her name—Jan or Jane, something with a *J*. She needs to schedule a psychiatrist appointment, so I can get something to help me sleep."

"I couldn't find her," I lie. I had meant to, but then, the orderlies. Of course I'm the daughter. *Of course.*

I catch sight of myself in the mirror across the room. I remember when Emily and I used to think thirty was ancient. *After forty*, she assured me at my thirty-first birthday. *That's when the years really catch up.*

It certainly feels true. There are faint lines around my eyes, a slight slackness in the skin around my jaw. Has there always been this much gray in my hair? I can feel my swollen calves, which my doctor told me was *chronic venous insufficiency*. There is a persistent ache in my neck, *arthritis*. A small scar on my forearm where a benign bump was removed, *basal cell carcinoma*. Signs that the body is not quite old, but youth is sure as hell receding. I look away when the Russian nurse comes in, holding a tray with Mom's dinner on it.

"Good evening, Mrs. Messing," she says, her accent thick.

Mom eyes her suspiciously. "I hope there's plenty of sauce this time." The nurse is polite and patient, even goes back to the kitchen to see if they have cracked pepper instead of the little packets.

While Mom eats she talks about the parties she and Dad

used to throw at the house. *Those were the days*, she says, sighing. Composers and producers; actresses like her and screenwriters like Dad, all of them vibrating with youth and beauty. *The world was going to be ours.* I readjust the napkin so that it covers a larger section of her blouse. *How cute the two of you were in your matching outfits*, she says about Emily and me. I refill her water cup, ask the nurse for more Parmesan cheese. *Everyone said I was crazy to have daughters so close in age, but I thought one could watch out for the other. And you were always so mature, so it worked out.* I dress her salad, tossing it with the flimsy plastic fork. *Do you remember demanding white wine spritzers at your twelfth birthday party?*

Yes. I nod. I have a different memory that I think of often. I must have been ten or twelve years old—it was around the time Emily started to look more and more like a bewitching little version of our mother, and everyone wanted to snap her picture or dress her up. It was easy to feel lost in the shuffle. But this memory. In it I'm dancing with a woman whose oversize bangles make her wrists look as delicate as bird bones. We are in the living room, in front of the big window facing the sea, and she is swaying her hips and motioning with her red lacquered nails for me to mimic her. Side to side, slower, slower. *As if you are kelp in the bay*, she says, the ocean big and blue behind her. *Move with the current.* And Guy is there—he is in all of my early memories. Like a fixture in the house. Part of the support beams holding it above the water. We danced like that for him. Me feeling a little naked and raw in my light cotton jumper but unwilling to stop because I liked the way he watched me, only me.

"I should throw a party when I get home. Doesn't that sound fun?" my mom says, stabbing a meatball with her fork.

I smile and wipe some sauce from her cheek. I don't point

out that most of her friends are dead. Or remind her that the house is split-level and nearly impossible for a woman in a walker to navigate, which is what she'll be needing when she leaves the nursing facility—and I definitely do not mention that I have been talking to a real estate broker since her hospitalization.

"It's not really such a bad place," she says, looking around the room. She's moved on to dessert. "They know how to make a decent rice pudding."

My hand shakes a little when I pour creamer into her coffee. If I got on a plane tonight I could be in Rome in time for dinner tomorrow. Homemade pasta, fresh tomatoes and basil. Real Parmesan cheese, not the kind that comes in packets. And wine—maybe something I haven't tasted before, a grape varietal I don't yet know. It would be nothing like here. A break from this place. From Mom. I want to get home and e-mail Paul. *I will be there. I am coming.*

I feel her eyes on me as I pack up my things.

"You should dye your hair before you leave," she says finally. "See if the salon can fit you in this week."

"That's a good idea." I kiss her goodbye.

"I bet Hannah is gorgeous, she'll look just like Emily did at that age. Beautiful, but not the brightest bulb. It's good you're going. You'll have to send me pictures."

She surveys my face. I try to keep it blank, unreadable. "Use my brightening mask when you get home. It'll clear up whatever's happening on your chin."

"I will." I shift my purse full of papers and snacks and bottled water from one shoulder to the other. "I love you, see you tomorrow."

I stop at the nurses' station and ask if the social worker can call me in the morning.

"She should be in her office," one of the nurses says.

"That's okay, a phone call is fine." I point toward my mom's room. "Also, could you make sure she gets a second rice pudding? She looks thin to me."

Outside, I take several deep breaths. It's twilight and the wind has picked up, shaking the palm trees and bougainvillea. Someone in the apartment complex next door is sautéing onions. I hear a baby crying; children are playing in the park across the street. Before I leave the parking lot, before I even turn the car on, I'm searching nonstop flights to Rome.

MONTI, ROME, ITALY

The boy's name is Donato. Short for Donatello. He's started to go by Donato only recently, his mother tells me. Her face is pinched pink with pleasure from talking about her only son.

"You know how boys are," she says. I nod as if I do. I watch him cross the room, his mother still beaming. He takes a pear from the kitchen table, tossing it up in the air and catching it. She fixes his flipped collar before he flops onto the couch.

"This year will be his last at Liceo Torquato Tasso." She gently pushes his feet from the throw pillows. "Then it will be on to the university." She says something to him in Italian that makes him throw up his arms, but then he smiles lovingly, mischievously at her. I feel a quick, unexpected pang of sadness.

I lean toward him. "What do you want to study?"

"He wants to be—" his mother interjects herself again. "How do you say?" Her English is good, but with a lilting accent. Like Fellini films, like postwar Italian actresses.

The boy motions to his limbs, makes a sleeping motion.

"Anesthesiologist," I tell him.

"*Sì.*" He smiles at me. It's a goofy, toothy grin. His nose is large and his ears stick out, but I like how his thick black hair gets in his eyes when he tilts his head to bite into the pear. He runs a hand through it to push it back, but it doesn't help.

There is a snap as he bites through the pear's skin, into the flesh, peeling it with his teeth. I watch his throat work as he eats. A bit of juice disappears beneath the collar of his shirt.

His mother huffs, pretending exasperation, and gets him a napkin. This is Paul and Hannah's apartment—Donato and his parents live one building over—but I can tell by how he stretches across the living room couch, how his mother directs my brother-in-law in the kitchen, that they might as well live here too.

"Marie's teaching me how to make a proper *cacio e pepe*," Paul calls to me from the stove. The pot of boiling water is making the room muggy. Marie goes to prop open the front door.

"You have not seen Hannah since her mamma's funeral?" Donato asks, watching me from the couch. He has very light brown eyes, fringed with thick lashes and full, almost feminine lips that are slick and shiny from the pear juice. I can feel him assessing me. Taking in the box-dye job, the blunt haircut I managed to fit in between visits to the nursing home and my red-eye flight. It's shorter than I wanted and feels uneven. *It looks exactly the same*, Guy assured me before dropping me off at the airport.

"Over a year now," I say, trying not to fidget.

He raises an eyebrow, still enjoying that pear.

I refuse to feel guilty. Paul had left for Italy soon after the funeral, taking Hannah with him. And I had my mother to think of, her grief was insurmountable. It affected everything. She did not want to go outside, she did not want to eat. Her health deteriorated and I had to stop working. What could I have told Hannah if I had called more? That for as long as she has been in Italy I have been my mother's full-time nurse? Or that last month, while picking up her medication, I got a phone call from the Malibu Fire Department saying she had tried to walk to the beach near our house and fallen, fracturing her pelvis and spraining her wrist? They were the ones to suggest a skilled nursing home facility, one nearby, somewhere I could visit.

I e-mailed when I found time. Made up stories about being on movie sets, tidbits about actors and actresses. Things I thought would entertain her. Hannah had been a mature child; an old soul like me. I think this, more than anything, caused the rift between Emily and me. That her only child took after me.

Before Emily got sick, the last time I'd been to their house was when she invited me to an award banquet in honor of Paul. *Please. I don't want to be around those university wives alone*, she said when she called. *They're so aggressive.* I was surprised, we hadn't been close for years, not since Dad died. But I went anyway, and of course Emily was completely in her element, the professors' wives all half envious and half in love with her. I had spent the better part of the night by her side, playing the role of big sister—champion and bodyguard—before I realized that she invited me not to give her support, but to bear witness to her greatness. To the spectacle of her in rare form. Queen even in a world that pooh-poohed Hollywood. *If religion is the opium of the people*, one of her tenured professor friends said within earshot of me, *then film is our partial lobotomy.*

Then, after the award was given, after the speeches, there was an intimate dinner at a nearby restaurant. Hannah got upset about where she was sitting, down at the end with the high chairs and toddlers—her face turned red and blotchy. I remember she smacked the table, knocking her glass over, spilling water everywhere. Emily was quick to get up and shield Hannah from the rest of us, putting her lithe body between her child and their friends. I watched the bent curve of her spine, was sure that she was first pacifying and then threatening, because that's what our mother would have done. Everything was for show. And it worked: when my sister moved away, Hannah had tucked her lip into her mouth, but gone were the hysterics.

"Aunt Cilla!" my niece cries from the front door. She drops her backpack on the floor and without kissing her father—who stood waiting, hopefully, in the kitchen, apron on, dirty dish towel over his shoulder—runs toward me, throwing her arms around my neck.

"Hello, sweetheart," I say. She is warm, a bit damp, and panting from the climb up the stairs. "Let me look at you."

The resemblance is startling. She's grown, nearly my height, slender and fair, her hair almost blond. My sister's eyes, deep blue, a little silvery too. The same dark brows, a similar sweetheart mouth and pert nose. It is utterly disarming. Something in my abdomen tightens. She is posing, letting me admire her. Then she bursts out laughing, hugging me again.

"Auntie, I am so glad you're here."

"Hannah," I say, squeezing her to me. "You're practically an adult."

She pulls away, keeping hold of my hand. "Please talk some sense into Papa."

Paul comes out from the kitchen. The apron's tied tight around his midsection, his fine hair combed back. "Cilla is here to help *me* with *you*."

She makes a face at him.

"Don't move me to Italy, where every goddamn person smokes, and not expect me to take it up."

"Language, *cucciola mia*," Donato's mother says.

Donato shoots up from where he's been watching, a teasing smile on his lips. He should be ungainly with such long limbs, but he crosses the room gracefully.

"Haahnaa," he says near her ear, flipping her ponytail. He tosses his pear core into the trash can.

She swats playfully at his passing hand.

"I don't care how young Italians start smoking," Paul says. "*My* daughter doesn't smoke. And she doesn't steal, either." He's trying to be tough. I can tell because he's giving his daughter the same look he sometimes gave my sister when she was alive. A look that says, I have authority, so won't you listen to me, please?

Donato is saying something to Hannah, in Italian maybe. It's too quiet to make out. Whatever it is, it makes her giggle.

"I'm so happy you're here," she says, turning her attention back to me. "Come and see my room."

The corridor is warmer and stuffier than the rest of the house, and I can feel the perspiration beneath my blouse. I hadn't expected Rome to be this hot; it's July and ninety degrees. There was a heat wave in Los Angeles when I left, record digits since late spring. Even in Malibu, where it can be twenty degrees cooler than the rest of the city, it was sweltering, the sun beat down; plants and people were shriveled and thirsty. But here in Rome the heat is different, cloying and leaden— crowded between buildings, *pressurized*. And the cicadas—the windows are closed, but still I can hear them, a constant din.

In Hannah's room she switches on the A/C unit. Watching her in her linen dress, I realize maybe I should have packed some dresses too. But there wasn't time to shop for new clothes. The haircut was squeezed in, and was probably a mistake. I should have left it long. I stand in front of the A/C unit, pulling my hair off my neck to let the skin there cool. Does it feel thinner? *It's probably just from stress*, the hairdresser tried to reassure me.

First, Hannah wants to show me her newest pair of strappy

platform sandals, then dresses and skirts she's bought from the boutiques along Via del Boschetto. She pulls out her phone and shows me pictures of girls she calls her "squad." Trish and Tina, two tall redheads, high shining foreheads, dotted with freckles; and a dark-haired girl, long-lashed, flashing a sultry look to the camera, a cigarette hanging from her lips. They look older than her, and in every photo, they have Hannah in the middle of them, as if she were a prized pet.

"You know, she's the one who got me into trouble?" Hannah says, sitting beside me on her bed. But I've lost which one she's talking about. I'm picturing Donato's smile, how he flipped her ponytail when he walked by. A finger brushing the back of her neck; just a quick knuckle against soft skin. I wonder if he could smell her shampoo when he flicked her hair, if that was why he had moved so close.

"I left a pack of cigarettes at her place, and when her mom found it she went absolutely apeshit. Trish had to tell her they were mine or her mother would probably have killed her."

Then she's up again. "Do you know what I really wanted to show you? It's here somewhere." She's pulling open drawers, humming to herself. Then she swings around. "Do you remember this?"

A gold-and-lapis pendant, the size of a silver dollar. I'd forgotten how '90s it looks, which I suppose is back in fashion. My niece has threaded it onto a gold chain, which she fastens around her neck. "I wish I had a picture of her wearing it."

Something to match the color of your eyes, our mom had said when she gave it to Emily for her sixteenth birthday. I found it just before Hannah left. Somehow it had made its way back into Mom's jewelry box. They were always sharing things. *Your mother wore it all the time when she was your age*, I had told Hannah. And I remember there hadn't been time to find a box, I had wrapped it in old tissue paper.

"Isn't this chain perfect?" my niece says, fingering it. "It's eighteen karat." The pendant glints in the light, and I'm reminded of all the times it flashed on my sister's jean jacket or smock dresses. I feel a little light-headed. Something about seeing this young version of my sister—with her confidence, her mannerisms. I am faintly nauseated, uneasy—like when I saw my mother in the hospital after her accident. Her white hair unruly, face gaunt, flat gray eyes. I couldn't tell if she was in there or not.

I shiver.

"Cold, Aunt Cilla? The humidity can do that here. God, I hate it."

"I'm just tired, I didn't sleep much on the plane."

She takes my arm. "Come on, let's go to your room, it's got a nicer view."

Watching the tanned backs of her legs climb the stairs two at a time, the thin curve of her ankles, her hair long and bouncing from each step, I feel more worn out than I should.

My room is rectangular and narrow, with a small A/C unit rattling above a writing desk, and a twin bed pushed against the opposite wall. Hannah has put a bouquet of daisies in a turquoise vase on the bedside table. My niece was right. The view is lovely. The large window faces the rear of the neighboring apartment buildings—their façades burnished yellow, gold, or orange. Their shutters in bold contrasting colors, all thrown open. Flowering vines droop down their sides, or hang from clay pots, large cumulus clouds cross the sky. Laundry lines swing in the breeze. Between the buildings, below us, is a courtyard, where a lemon tree rests in the center, ripe with fruit.

"It must feel like living in a film," I tell her, my body half out the window. The color of the sky—I can't imagine what a lighting director would have to do to get that sheen, that sharp golden glow. I feel a flutter of excitement; Los Angeles is so far away.

My niece plops onto the bed. "It's fine. I wish Papa wasn't so strict. He won't even let me go out to dinner with you guys tonight."

I turn from the window, remembering why I'm here. "Don't you have a make-up exam early in the morning?"

She gives me the same look Emily did when she was caught, guilty but about to make an excuse. She's probably gotten away with just about anything, up until now. But I know all my sister's tricks.

"He's down there making dinner for you," I tell her. "We'll have plenty of time to catch up—as long as you stay on top of your studies."

I sit with her on the bed that will be mine until Hannah's Italian class is over. Then we'll escape the sweltering city for Puglia, where the two families have rented rooms at a *masseria* on a working olive farm.

"How is your Italian?" I ask.

She sighs and says something I don't understand at all.

"Souhds fluent to me." I laugh.

"I don't know why he moved us here. I miss . . ." She stops.

I think, *Please don't say it*. I'm exhausted. My head is pounding. And she doesn't.

She must see my relief as some sort of shared pain, because she gives me a quick kiss and tells me she's so happy I'm here, that we're going to have so much fun.

"Even if I do have stupid Italian class every day." Her pout is exactly like her mother's, and for a moment I think she might be Emily incarnate.

I manage to tell her something comforting—about picking her up from class, how she can show me the best gelato shops. "If I don't gain ten pounds, I'll consider this trip a failure."

She laughs and takes out a pack of cigarettes. "You don't mind if I smoke, do you, Aunt Cilla?"

"Yes, I definitely mind," I say, taking the pack from her. "Your grandmother is on oxygen because of these things." Hannah purses her lips but doesn't object, just drops onto the bed, stretching her slim arms and legs. "And let's please drop the 'Auntie,' it makes me feel old. Cilla is fine."

"How's Guy?" she asks, sighing. "He's so cool. Dad says he's directing now. Have you been on any good sets lately? Seen any movie stars?"

"Nothing new since my last e-mail," I say, and when she looks disappointed I add something about lunch at the Chateau Marmont, about running into the actress Sarah Paulson. "From the *American Horror Story* series."

"I never really got into that show."

I swallow. She's spreading her hair across the bedspread. I want to say something closer to the truth, something other than a silly lie.

"Your grandmother sends her love."

"You know," she says, not hearing me. Her hair looks thicker fanned out like that, like the mane of an animal. "Donato tells his parents he wants to be a doctor, but really, he wants to be a movie star."

———

In the cab ride from the airport we crossed the Tiber, which was wilder than I imagined, scruff growing up around its edges, not a boat on it. Hannah said that at night, clubs open right on its banks. *You can walk up or down a mile and go to fifteen different bars*, she said before leaving so I could take a nap. Then she bounced right back in with an adapter for my phone charger and more questions about the trip. *Later, darling, later.* I nearly pushed her into the hall.

I take three Advils, and also zinc because the child next to me on the plane had a runny nose. My cheeks are flushed despite the A/C cooling the room. I wash my face and administer various toners and moisturizers and antiwrinkle creams. I do the facial yoga exercises I looked up after leaving the nursing facility that day. *Do I really look like I could be Mom's sister?* I look exhausted. But who wouldn't after a long flight?

I think about when Emily was pregnant with Hannah, how at first, she was rosy and plump. She looked electric. Like in a film, when every scene is dreary, blue and gray, and then the starlet walks in emitting a vibrant buttery glow. That's how it was. I picture her smiling, one hand on her belly, telling Mom and me the good news.

I think I hear Donato's voice, and then the front door to the apartment opens and shuts. I can make out every one of his footsteps on the stairs. I wait at the bedroom window, which is actually quite large. I could climb right out of it if I wanted. Perch out there on the roof tiles, taking in that lush golden sky. A figure wrapped in a robe moves from room to room in a neighboring building. Below in the courtyard a black cat dozes beneath the lemon tree.

Across the way, almost exactly opposite, a light switches on. I wonder if this is where Donato lives with his parents. I can still hear Marie downstairs in the kitchen with Paul. She's acting as secretary to Paul and her husband, Tonio, while they work on their book focused on Roman funerary art. They are researching votive offerings from the Augustan age. The most exciting find, Paul had rattled on when we spoke on the phone—and why he couldn't let up on his research, why he needed my help—was their discovery of the most ancient remains of lemon ever found in the Mediterranean. *It's extraordinary*, he said, breathless.

No wonder Hannah was acting out.

My phone vibrates, starting to turn on. There's a text from Guy: *Safe Travels!* ✈

I lie down on the bed, a nap before a late dinner with the rest of the adults—Paul, Marie, Tonio, and me. *They eat late in Rome*, Paul had said. *Our reservations are at nine. Take a nap, I've got to finish this pasta for Hannah.* A good man, my brother-in-law. When he and Emily met, he had been giving a talk at NYU on ancient cities' influence on modern city planning. Somehow, randomly, Emily was there. An unlikely love story. Paul, a distinguished visiting scholar, with his easy demeanor and unassuming features—brown eyes, small nose, and long face. And Emily, a failed model living in a swanky Sober Living apartment in Manhattan, which our parents were paying for. *I was the most beautiful ruin he'd ever seen*, my sister joked when they came to visit. Paul, who by this time had moved to the States to be with her, blushed and kissed her hand. *I'm the lucky one*, he replied. A good man. It circles in my head like that as I dial Guy, my phone pressed against my ear. *A-good-man. A-good-man.*

When Guy answers I think I can hear the commotion of being on set, the dropping of equipment, the gruff barking of the set builders, the light, cautious voices of the PAs, someone nearby, who Guy shouts at to *Take over*. Then he's somewhere quiet, his stage office probably, I hear a door shut. I think, *No, no, go back, I miss those sounds most.*

"Hiya, babe, how's it going? How was the flight?"

"Fine and fine. Hannah looks so much like Emily, it's unnerving."

I can tell he's smiling; I can always tell when Guy's smiling.

"How's Mom?" I ask.

I listen to his account of going by the nursing home this morning, making sure she is eating the oranges I gathered from the tree in our courtyard.

"She said the guy in room eight has been hitting on her," he says.

"You can't believe anything she says. She thinks *everyone's* flirting with her—the doctor, the other patients, even the nurses. The woman is relentless."

He laughs, sounding like an old man. I think of those long-ago parties—the cigarettes and joints, making sure there were glasses of water and Advil on my parents' bedside tables, microwaving mac and cheese for Emily, making sure she showered and brushed her teeth. I see Guy sitting on our living room couch, younger than my parents and their friends but so much older than me. My father's protégé. Always the last to leave, still awake when everyone else was in bed. *Someone needs to take care of you*, he would say, helping me empty the ashtrays, loading the dishwasher. I think of my fifteenth birthday, when he said I looked like a young Jane Fonda and tucked a flower into the bosom of my dress, and I thought to myself, not for the first time, *I'd let him kiss me.*

Soon after, he made his first move. Climbing up my leg, his thumb pressing against my underwear, against that soft warmth. He touched and I watched spellbound—his mouth droop open, his other hand undoing his belt. I watched as he stroked, almost pumping, teeth gritted. Telling me, *Hush, hush, don't make a sound.* The housekeeper's voice coming from just outside the garage, the laundry room probably. *Cilla? Cilla? Where is Cilla? Pricillaaa*—wait, no, that was Guy's voice when he came.

"Pricilla, are you there? I said, what do you think of Rome?"

I roll onto my side, pulling the pillow lengthwise, squeezing it into me.

"It's like a set come to life."

"Ha. If you think about it, every other city is the set version of Rome. You're in the real one. It must be a trip."

"I guess so." But I can't seem to wrap my head around what he's getting at. I must be more jet-lagged than I thought.

Los Angeles, New York, America . . . all pretend.

I drift off again, lulled by his voice.

"Is Hannah going to be as much trouble as Emily?" I jerk awake at the sound of her name coming out of his mouth. "And Paul, how's he doing, the old sap?"

"A little aged, but then, we're all older now. We're going out to dinner pretty soon."

He laughs again. "Ah, Italian eating hours. Lucky girl. You'll come home big as a house."

"Like you can talk," I tease.

This makes him laugh harder, the deep self-assured boom of a man who's done well for himself. *He'll never make it as a writer*, Dad used to say, *but man, can that boy talk.*

Guy was my first everything. Limb to limb, sweat to sweat, every crevice explored. He only had to peer at my bare legs and I knew how it would end—in my parents' bed when they were away, in the backyard, the back of his car, once on a studio jet. Everywhere. In my twenties he took me out to clubs, to gaudy, expensive restaurants, which dazzled me at the time. He liked to show me off, I think. But over the years the sex changed, became more caressing, more patient. In my thirties I thought he would finally propose. I thought, *Enough of this charade, make it official.* At the very least, *Stop messing around with those puerile wannabe actresses, and let's be exclusive.* It was like that, my entire thirties. Waiting.

"Did you go by the house?" I ask.

"Yes, and I got the estimate from the exterminator. I don't know why you want to sell. You won't be able to find anything like it. Not to mention your mom will never let you do it."

I ignore him and pull up the calendar on my laptop, note the price and day the exterminator can tent the house. I ask if I need to call, or if Guy can handle it for me.

"Mom is going to have to accept how things are," I tell him. "Having a split-level beach house when you're using a walker isn't feasible."

It wasn't until I was living there alone that the idea of selling became appealing. A house empty of people is not the same thing as an empty house. It is filled with ghosts. Mom's stuff overflowing her walk-in closet, Dad's collection of glassware undusted in the living room—what once was Chanel No. 5 and Nat Sherman cigarettes is now the chalky whiff of dust, the musty smell of mildew. And Emily—in her porcelain urn on the living room mantel, blocking the view of the Pacific. At night it takes on a bluish hue from the moon, as if glowing from within.

"Why don't you remodel, and then rent out one of the floors as a guesthouse? You know if you sell, it'll be torn down. They'll build one of those mega-mansions."

I bite my lip. I wouldn't be able stand that, and Guy knows it. Before Mom's fall I had been making progress in the garden. Pinching and pruning, removing the spent flowers from the globe mallow, trying to untangle the mess of honeysuckle vines, cutting back the lavender and sprays of purple sage. It might have been enough. To have my own garden. At least, that's what I like to think.

"Besides, where will you go? Anywhere other than LA and you'll be all alone."

"Please," I say, getting up to turn the A/C higher. "Let's talk about something else."

He clears his throat. "Actually, I did want to talk to you about something."

I imagine Guy settling into a broad leather couch. He never sits at a desk, always the couch, where there is room for two. Knees apart, leaning back slightly so his belt buckle catches the light. Like the starting point on a map. YOU ARE HERE.

I feel a flush creeping into my cheeks. My hair is sticking to my neck. This bloom of heat has been happening more and more. I don't like to think of what it means. Instead I try to picture Guy. He isn't unattractive. Average height, with salt-and-pepper hair cut military short, strong features but a weak round chin. I've always been partial to his eyes, which are blue like the bottom of a pool in summer, the corners tilting down making him look a little like Bogart.

"It's about Trudy," he's saying. Heat explodes at her name and I am on fire. "I know, I know, you advised against casting her." He starts listing how wonderful she was in her last guest-starring role, how he thinks she's the next *real* thing.

"I think I advised against casting with your dick," I snap.

Immediately I'm frustrated with myself for getting upset. I get up, pulling my top off, and push the window open. I feel my nipples harden under my bra from the sudden gust of warm air. I take a deep steadying breath. "I'm sorry, I'm just looking out for your production, like any producer would."

He doesn't remind me that I am not actually on the project,

only a trusted confidant. And if I want to remain so, I'll give him what he's asking for, which is my approval.

I hear him shift, the leather beneath him groaning. "I don't care if it's a small role," he says. "No, I do, it needs to have lines. She wants to have lines."

I had dinner with them the night before I flew out. Trudy, rail thin and young—they're always young. If I squinted she looked like all the others. Dripping in newly bought couture, from Guy, I'm sure. It had been the same when I was her age— but could I have ever been *that* young? Baby fat still in the cheeks, her fur coat slipping from one shoulder, exposing dewy skin. I had kept my cardigan on, even though it was a warm night, even though I've always been rigorous in my workouts: Pilates and cycling, an occasional boot camp if I can get away from Mom. My arms are nothing to be ashamed of, is what I'm saying. But skin changes after forty. It doesn't matter if I eat right or buy the expensive creams. Little bumps, unsightly moles, skin tags. Burn it, slice it, *get it off.* But it's never the same, it's never how it used to be.

"Why ask my opinion anyway?" I get up to pour water from a pitcher Hannah or Paul has left on the dresser, the ice already melted. "I've been out of the business too long."

"Don't start that," he says. "When you're ready, there's a job for you. I've always said that. I owe your family a lot."

You owe me *a lot*, I think. But don't say it. I never say it. He promises to continue visiting my mom, and to call this weekend. I make a kiss-kiss sound before hanging up, telling him to give my love to Trudy. We both know it's insincere, but this is how it is between us.

It's not yet seven, the light over the buildings is gray and balmy. Somewhere someone is smoking, I can smell it. But then there is Donato, standing below in the shadowed courtyard.

I recognize the mop of unruly curls. Someone joins him. I squint against the fading light—I know that linen dress, the blond hair. I step back when she looks up. When I peer out again, she's taken his cigarette. He steps closer to her—is that her giggle? But it's lost in the surrounding city noise. A trash truck, glass bottles dropping, a dog barking, somewhere music is playing. And then she's handing the cigarette to Donato, who puts it between his lips and watches her dash inside. He catches me then, a quick glance up, the ember of his cigarette sparking bright red.

—

I have a hard time sleeping, the dim light plays tricks on me. There is a flapping of wings, flashes of shadow along the wall. More than once I jerk awake to an empty room, the hum of medical equipment replaced with the buzz of cicadas. Starlings cry out somewhere in the city, like shrieking children. Downstairs, tableware clatters onto the kitchen floor. When I do drift off, it's a deep sleep, and Emily is there. She is thirty-nine, skin alabaster white, so unlike my own, which is tawny and freckled. She's running into the ocean by our house. I can see her long, lean back, the flare of her hips and buttocks, the slender curved legs—*bowlegged*—something she was insecure about, which cut her modeling career short. The ocean is not blue, but black, with froth as white as her skin. And it consumes my sister, just eats her up. Then she's gone, and I wake in a puddle of my own sweat.

When I come downstairs, we're already running late for our reservation, and Tonio, Donato's father, doesn't arrive until we are about to leave without him.

"Research," Paul tells me. "We are onto something big."

Tonio says several things in Italian, his sentences running together, his hand running absently over his neatly trimmed silvery beard. "Sorry," he says to me, smiling a little. "I will try to speak in English."

He's much older than his wife, Marie, who must be in her thirties. He has a solid, broad frame, and is even darker than Donato, who is olive-skinned like his mother. They look nothing alike—although when Tonio turns in profile to greet his son, and they are side by side, there is the same jaw, a similar squareness in the shoulders. A hint of the man Donato may grow into.

Outside, the streets are pulsing with energy. It rained while I slept, and the whole city glistens. That tingle of excitement returns. There are people everywhere. The men in expensive khakis and linen jackets mop their foreheads, while trying to attend to their dates, whose heels keep slipping on the slick cobblestone street. Tour groups strain to keep from getting separated. Students crowd the cafés and bars, music spilling out onto the street. Old people sit on their balconies, fanning themselves slowly. Taxis and mopeds attempt to push through the foot traffic. A cyclist with a glaring headlamp races by.

Marie walks with her son, oblivious to the commotion. They are arm in arm, she is almost the perfect height to rest her head on his shoulder. Even in tortoiseshell glasses, her thick hair pulled up in a chignon, she looks very young. She's dressed conservatively, a mid-length, pale yellow dress with a linen shawl wrapped around her shoulders. I walk with them, only so I don't have to try to keep up with Tonio and Paul, who are ahead of us, deep in conversation.

"Did you have a nice rest?" Donato asks me.

I have not shaken the feeling of sleep, and with the gas lamps flickering along the stone walls and narrow streets, the scent of rain somewhere in the distance, I could be dreaming still. It's as if Rome wants to win the part of Ancient City. Just the slant of the trees seems artificial, like props in a diorama. And then the stone walls and arches and roads all there to evoke poetic tragedy. It reminds me of a carefully curated head shot of a woman made to look like the girl next door, or the seductress, or whatever the part demanded.

"It was a very long flight," I say. "I think I could have slept for a week."

He pulls me toward him, just in time. A moped speeds by.

"Are you all right?" Marie says to me. Donato yells after the driver in Italian, still holding my arm.

We turn down a walkway so crowded that Marie is forced to let go of her son. We walk in single file past street peddlers who offer us purses and toys and cheap souvenirs. I pass a hunk of meat slowly rotating on a spit; the smell is thick and earthy. I've slowed to watch a man carefully shave off thin slices—the knife cutting right through, severing it as if it were a tender limb.

"Sorry," Donato says, bumping into me.

I smile at him, which makes him smile too.

"Stay close," he says. "There are pickpockets."

"I've read that, is it true?"

"When my friends and I were younger, we used to pick tourists' pockets for fun, just so they know whose city they are in." His smile has changed, an eyebrow has gone up, he looks sideways at me to see if I believe this.

"You're messing with me," I say.

It's the first time I hear him laugh, openmouthed and unabashed.

"Guess you will never know."

He's so young and confident that something inside me

bristles. I'd like to see him bend, if only a little, and I remember what Hannah told me.

"You know, with that profile you could be an actor."

He stops laughing. "You think so?" He turns so I can admire his broad nose and chin; his ink-black hair, curly like his mother's. I wish I hadn't said it, because I realize it's true. He is handsome yet boyish, infuriatingly so. The studios would love him.

He lets out that laugh again, only this one isn't at my expense. "Hollywood," he says, blushing a little. "I've always wanted to go." He casts a furtive glance toward his parents, who are a few steps ahead of us. "My parents would not like it."

I shrug. "Well, you've got that special something."

He's so pleased that when we catch up to his mother he gives her one arm, and me the other.

A group of boys are waiting for him outside the restaurant. All of them in stylish suit coats, deep V-neck T-shirts, hair immaculate, slick and shining. Donato breaks from his mother and me and joins them. There's an eruption of boyish energy, of handshakes and laughing and cigarette lighting.

"They are going to Club Fluid," Marie tells me. "One of his friends is co-owner." Donato jogs back to us. He bends to kiss his mother goodbye, tossing me a wink before rejoining his friends.

At dinner Paul orders the fried artichokes and a tahini plate to start, with a bottle of Verdicchio, later a bottle of red with the pasta and meat dishes—ravioli with meat sauce, baked lamb and potatoes, *Amatriciana alla giudia*. "You're in for a treat," he tells me. "Best in Rome, they use salted beef instead of guanciale."

The conversation is limp, boring. Tonio asks how my flight was, then Paul inquires what airline miles card I use. Marie suggests I switch to this other credit card, telling me how much they've saved. The waiter keeps refilling my wineglass. We are seated next to the open window, thank goodness. There is a warm, gentle wind, blowing the thunderclouds out. I think of Donato and his friends at Club Fluid. I can picture the lighting, the dancing—girls will flock to them, I'm sure. When Donato had taken my arm, I caught a smell of aftershave. But his face was so smooth, shaving would be unnecessary. For a moment, I'd wanted to inspect him closer, run my fingers over his cheeks, along his jaw.

"Are you feeling okay?" Paul asks. Marie and Tonio are looking at me. "You look a little flushed."

I realize I've started to sweat under my arms—I feel it drip onto my stomach. My hands are bright red. "It's warm in here, is all." I'm having trouble slipping my cardigan off, Paul helps me with it.

"Maybe you're allergic to sulfates," he suggests.

The waiter comes over and opens the window wider. The city smells dank, like compost, like the decomposing of something rich and fertile, layers and layers and layers of it.

"What was I saying?" I pause to sip my ice water. I've lost the thread of my story. I had been telling Marie and Tonio about Emily and Paul's wedding. "Well, it was gorgeous." I smile at Marie. "The prettiest wedding I've been to. It was at the Beverly Hills Hotel. Marilyn Monroe once lived in one of the bungalows."

Marie sighs, touches her hand to her chest.

I leave out how dazzling my sister had been in Vera Wang, her creamy white skin, those deep blue eyes, the blond curl that had escaped from her updo and rested on her cheek. Friends, distant relatives, neighbors, colleagues—my mother invited everyone. I think she wanted them to see how Emily had bounced back, that a celebrated academic obviously adored her. I remember Paul's small gasp when she appeared in her wedding dress. It wasn't loud, I might have been the only one to hear it, everyone else was paying attention to the bride. But I heard the sharp intake of breath, saw how he pressed his lips tight, trying not to cry. One untrimmed nose hair waving haphazardly with each inhalation.

He makes me laugh, my sister said when I asked what it was that had attracted her to him. *And he loves me.* At her urging he left Oxford for a university in Irvine; they bought a house in San Clemente near a stretch of beach my sister had always liked. He took a leave of absence when she got sick that first time. Driving her to chemo and doctor appointments, taking care of Hannah, who was only a toddler then. And when she was declared in remission they went on a celebratory trip to France. Mom framed the postcard she sent from Paris, my sister's lip print smeared from having traveled so far.

The second time, though—when it came back years later and was determined to be terminal—Paul was devastated. The kind of clueless devastation that only an intelligent man can have. He buried himself in a new research project, made contact with a professor at Sapienza, the top university in Rome, who turned out to be Tonio, and who would later, after my sister's death, help secure Paul a research position.

I glance at my brother-in-law. During my retelling of his wedding he smiled and nodded and laughed at all the right parts, but I couldn't tell if he had gotten choked up or if the *Amatriciana alla giudia* had really been as spicy as he proclaimed. He looks wistful now, staring blankly at his plate, napkin clutched in his hand, ready to dab at his eyes again if needed.

"It's very warm in here," I say to myself, realizing I'm a bit drunk, and so hot that I've started using my cloth napkin to wipe at my forehead. Is this a hot flash? A similar wave of heat had hit me while the doctor at the hospital had been telling me about Mom's condition. He could see that I had sweated through my dress, the beads of perspiration at my temples. *Would you like to sit down, Ms. Messing?* That first night I was alone in our house, I drank a bottle of Viognier and read articles on WebMD. I watched a well-produced video of a dancing uterus and ovaries sing about hair loss and fertility declining after thirty. I ordered something called a perimenopause diary but could not get past the first couple pages. *Mood swings, hot flashes, night sweats, insomnia, hair loss, sore swollen breasts, pimples, vaginal dryness.* There had been columns for each. *Rate from 1–10.*

Does it matter? Mom had said when I asked how old she was when she started menopause. *Everything's downhill after thirty-five.*

When the wine was gone I was too scared to go downstairs for another bottle. Our house felt haunted. I jumped at any strange noises—crows outside, the water heater switching on. A dog barking in the alley. I smoked a partially crushed joint that Guy left the last time he was over, and passed out watching reruns of the sitcom I co-produced with him in my thirties.

I run my hand over my neck, feeling my glands, imagining where my thyroid might be. I'll find a specialist when I go home, maybe consult an acupuncturist or a nutritionist. There must be something to prevent menopause, just for a little while longer. I have not done enough, there hasn't been sufficient time. Men are lucky. I watch Tonio talking, so distinguished with the silver in his beard and at his temples, the gently wrinkled forehead. I think of Guy, ordering the film crew around, how this always impresses the starlets. I imagine Donato at the club with his friends. The world makes room for them at any age.

The meat dishes come, the lamb stewed in its own juices, the potatoes are tender and bright yellow. I don't need a knife, but the waiter brings big serious-looking ones with serrated silver blades.

I can tell Marie is interested in stories about Hollywood, but Tonio, when I bring up my first film, really my father's final movie, fidgets in his seat, cuts through his meat so that the knife screeches against the plate.

"*Mi dispiace*," he says without looking up. He reaches for the bottle of wine, but Paul is there first, offering Marie some, and then me.

"It must be very glamorous," Marie says.

Tonio lets his silverware drop on his plate. He says something quickly to his wife in Italian.

For dessert Paul orders a mixed berry gelato, and without asking, espresso for Marie, and grappa for himself and Tonio.

"An espresso for me too," I tell the waiter, who is turning away.

"Oh! I'm sorry," Paul says, touching my arm. "We're so used to going out the three of us. Do you want anything else? A grappa? Cheese plate?"

"No, please," I say, looking at the waiter and Paul. "Only the espresso, I'm about to fall asleep in my chair. I could not eat another bite. Everything was delicious."

"We should have done this tomorrow," Paul says. "But I wanted so badly to take you out tonight. To do Rome right on your first night here. Isn't it the most beautiful city you've ever seen? I mean, look right there—those stumps around the patio tables, do you see them? That's what's left of three hundred columns, once the Porticus of Octavia, built in 146 BC, reconstructed by Augustus in 23 BC, then again two hundred and thirty years later." Paul is really excited now. The grappa has arrived, and he twists the stem of the tiny glass. The candlelight dapples his face with light and shadow. "We are living here, Cilla. Ghosts and all."

—

The nurse sounds annoyed when I call.

"Is it very late?" I hear methodic beeping, hushed talking.

I had woken up early. Or maybe I hadn't slept at all, only hovered on the surface, like floating on the ocean at home with Emily. We used to swim naked at night. Stripping down and running out, hopping over the sand crabs and pebbles and pieces of shells. We'd swim past the surf, the tangles of seaweed, Emily braver than I. She'd swim farther and farther, urging me to follow her into the dark.

"It's nearly nine o'clock, Ms. Messing. Your mother is asleep already."

I push open the bedroom window; the light outside is graying. Seagulls are nesting on the roof across the courtyard. One begins to call.

I try to place the accent. "Is this Olga?"

"Doris, ma'am."

"How is she doing? Has she been behaving herself?" I picture the nursing home, its looped hallway silent except for the few patients who prefer to stay up at night. Dad was like that, always refusing to sleep. At night he would not stay in bed. He sat in the community room or the physical therapy room, or roamed the halls in his wheelchair, nodding off and then lurching awake. We'd get phone calls in the middle of the night, Dad on the other end whispering about nursing home conspiracies, demanding that Mom come and get him. I started keeping the house phone with me so I could intercept the calls.

Is that you, Cilla, sweetheart? Please, please, come and get me. Please. It's the pleading I remember most.

"She was in a good mood today, we're starting physical therapy next week. Do you want me to have the doctor phone you with an update?"

"Yes, thank you. Tell her I'll call in the morning to say hello."

"I'm sure she'll like that. Good night, Ms. Messing."

I lie down on the bed, watching the light outside grow brighter and brighter. Car sounds increase, construction noises commence. The temperature shifts, becomes heavier, warmer. Somewhere a siren begins to wail. It sounds obscured, though, like a muffled voice track on a bad recording. I must fall back to sleep, because suddenly there is a knock at the bedroom door and my niece bounds into the room.

"*Buongiorno!*" She plops down on the foot of the bed. I can smell her lotion, which has some kind of florally perfume. "We left you coffee and breakfast downstairs. See you at two, okay? Two o'clock, don't forget."

I struggle to sit up.

"Wow, you are not a morning person," she says, reaching out to fix my hair. "Mom was like that too. I have a hair mask in my bathroom, it'll help repair this. It's made with avocado."

Downstairs I hear Paul call for her.

"Be right there!" she yells.

"Hannah, please," I say. "Not so loud."

"Two o'clock, okay? Don't be late, I have so much planned for us."

She's wearing sparkly blue eye shadow, her blond hair straightened so that it frames her face.

"I'll be there at two sharp, I promise."

She gives me a kiss, and then bounces downstairs. I listen

until the commotion ceases, until the front door shuts and the bolt locks.

On the kitchen counter Paul's left a note with Hannah's school address, which is near the Piazza del Popolo, and a list of phone numbers if I should need to get ahold of him. He will be at the university until late tonight.

I pour a cup of coffee and start to inspect the kitchen cupboards. Note the expired tub of yogurt, the leaky box of kosher salt, the almost empty bowl of sugar. Emily would never have had sugar in the house. Not long after Hannah was born, she started to make her own herbal teas and salves. Soon she forbade anything processed; everything had to be homemade. It was maddening how self-righteous she was about it. If someone complained of an ailment, there was some elixir made from elderberry or turmeric that would help. Once she brought over carrot soup to help with Dad's macular degeneration. Never mind that he'd have to eat a couple pounds' worth of carrots to get any real nutritional value from them.

In Hannah's bathroom I find an old dried tube of toothpaste, next to a disgusting hairbrush—a hunk of long blond hairs with bits of frizz and dandruff. I decide to buy her another one this afternoon and throw it out.

It's warm again, but early enough that there's cloud cover. I don't know what had me spooked the night before, but in the morning light, Monti is a charming little neighborhood, perfect for a green-screen backdrop. Boxed geraniums hang from balconies, a fountain gurgles in the piazza. The crush of tourists has not yet descended and I'm able to walk through the streets easily. A shop owner props open her door, nodding to me, *Buongiorno!* There is the whirring of an espresso machine, the racket of cups and spoons and plates coming from a café. Pigeons in the street fly off when a cab whizzes by.

By the time I get to the Roman Forum there are tour groups everywhere and the sun is beating down. Italian, English, French, Chinese, Russian. I'm almost trampled by a large German family, their towheaded children nearly shoving me out of line. I check my ticket for what must be the fiftieth time. I bought it while still in Los Angeles, thinking it wise to plan in advance. But the website's translation was confusing and difficult to navigate. The entry time on the ticket says 00:00, which can't be right, that would mean midnight. I tried calling but couldn't get through. When it's my turn at the box office window, I show the printed ticket to the woman. Try to explain my dilemma.

"It doesn't make sense," I say, as she blinks at me. She's probably around my age but with a stylish neckerchief and a pretty clip in her thick undyed hair. "I chose nine thirty on the website, not midnight."

She stares at me blankly. "I'm sorry, do you understand?" I swallow. "I don't speak Italian."

She looks at the paper, then smiles, chuckling. "Do not worry," she says, waving her hand. "You have a ticket, you go in." She's still smiling that mysterious smile. This must happen all day, I realize. She hears the accent and thinks, ah, another American with their life mapped out to the minute. Not here. Not in Rome. *Do not worry*. As if timetables and tickets and planning in advance were trivial, silly things.

"*Scusa*," a mother behind me says, tugging on her child's arm. She steps in front of me.

Inside, the ruins seem sculpted. I'm suspicious of the flowers growing between crumbling brick, it looks entirely too picturesque. It can't be real. A good set designer could make a more believable ruin than this.

I've followed my tour book into a dead end, somewhere not

on the map. It's sweltering now, the cicadas at full pitch. I take a break on a slab of stone with vines growing on a nearby wall like shaggy mops of hair. A pair of white butterflies float down, almost resting on the vines, and then back up, they flit away. I try to let go and be present for this moment.

Where should I go for lunch after this? I use my phone to see if the restaurants I marked in my book are nearby. Should I call and make a reservation? And Mom, what time should I call her? *Do not worry*, I hear that woman from the box office say. She said it as if absolving me of something. Guy had said that every city is the set version of Rome. Maybe that has something to do with it. Living in a city that's not made in the image of any other, she knows what's important and what isn't. There had been a similar unhurried vibe at dinner last night, as if it could have stretched on forever.

I close my eyes. Within a minute I've listed five things to ask the doctor when he calls with an update on Mom's condition. I open my eyes and snap a picture of my sandaled feet standing on the broken stone floor, proof that I was here. But the toes in the photo look dry and ugly. I delete it.

Nearby, a couple is wrapped in an embrace. I can't tell their age—younger than Donato and his friends. This is no PG embrace either, she is nearly straddling him, her hands in his hair. I can see him working his tongue into her mouth, the movement his hand is making under her skirt. I hear a moan escape from one of them and look away. It's been a long time since I've been that girl. Or maybe I've never been her. I sneak another look, just to note how she's slouched a little, her eyes shut.

They break apart just as a noisy tour group enters the small alcove.

"Those vestal virgins found guilty of being unchaste"—their

41

leader's voice ricochets off the surrounding walls—"were whipped to death in the public square." She pauses so they can take photos and ask questions. "Public deaths were popular," I hear her answer someone. "As were blood shows—known as *munera*. After lunch we will see the slave quarters beneath the Colosseum."

There are collective *oohhs* and *aahhs*, and I wonder if they would watch one, or if I would. The ripping of flesh, the breaking of man. Suddenly I get a cramp. When was the last time I had my period? Three, five weeks ago? I can't remember. I should have been recording it in that damn diary.

One of the tour members is watching the couple, who are back at it. Our eyes meet, and I feel myself blush. He's short and hefty, wearing pleated pants and a sweat-stained polo shirt. His hand rests on a camera that hangs around his neck. He smiles, waggles his eyebrows. Yes, hi, hello. I give him a polite grimace and turn so I can sit more comfortably. Then slowly, out of the corner of my eye I see him raise his camera and click. I don't know if he's taking a picture of me or the couple or the ruins. Maybe all three.

When the cramp subsides, the tour has moved on. The couple too. At the entrance, I flag down a cab, feeling more spent than I should.

"*Signora, signora.*" The cabby rattles off something in Italian.

Usually a migraine precedes my period, and I think I feel one coming on.

"Where to?" he finally asks in English.

"Somewhere quiet, please," I tell him as I roll up the window. I want to shut out those tourists, that young kissing couple, that horrible little man. It's too early to wait in the piazza for Hannah, and I don't want to go back to the apartment, to that small narrow bedroom. That would be like giving up. I imagine the woman at the box office would disapprove. *Do not worry.*

"Somewhere quiet," I repeat again, rubbing my temples. "Somewhere near the Piazza del Popolo, but not the Piazza del Popolo."

I don't know if he understands me or not, but he nods and rolls the rest of the windows up, switching on the air conditioner to full blast.

———

"Villa Borghese," the cabdriver says, and he gives me two thumbs up. I pay him, probably tipping too much, because his smile is very big as he pulls away.

It's an expansive park, with grassy acres, overgrown plane trees and stone pines making it look unkempt. Tourists roll by on Segways, others pedal tandem bikes. A family rests beside a fountain. I watch the mother cup water and motion for her sons to drink. They're obedient, both of them shirtless and scrawny. I can see every bump and ridge in their spines, like a delicate string of beads. There is pleasure and joy in the mother's face. When they're finished they clatter onto their bikes and ride away.

The path I take leads to a large empty space, no trees or structures or anything. Not a plaque to explain what it was once for. There are a few people throwing balls for dogs, but I can't imagine ancient Rome having a dog park.

One of the dog owners looks over. He's far away, but I can tell from the tilt of his head, from the full laugh, that it's Donato.

I see him wave, a small dog jumping at his legs. For some

reason, I sit on a bench and pretend to look through my guide-book.

When he reaches me he says, "Cilla, ciao!"

"Donato." I look up, feigning surprise.

He bends to kiss my cheek. His lips are as soft as they look. When I move away he still has hold of my arm.

"In Italy we kiss twice," he says, and pulls me in again.

"Oh, right." I fumble for his other cheek. "Ciao," I say, try-ing to ignore how much pleasure he is taking from befud-dling me.

"Are you here alone?" he asks, grinning.

"I came from the Forum, I'm meeting Hannah soon."

The dog, a brown-and-white Jack Russell, paws at my legs, whimpering.

"No, Bruce, no," he says, pulling on the leash. "I watch him for a friend while she is at work."

"Hello you, hello." I pet the dog until it's settled down. "Why did she name him Bruce?"

He pantomimes a machine gun. "Yippee-ki-yay, mother-fucker!"

"After Bruce Willis. Nice guy, by the way. Swell."

Swell? Who talks like that? I bet his mother doesn't use whatever the equivalent in Italian is.

He's sat down now, his hands in his lap. He's wearing a striped collared shirt, the collar undone, sleeves rolled up. It's the first time I notice his hands, which look older than the rest of him—dried and cracked around the knuckles, long knobby fingers, narrow delicate wrists. And his forearms, have I ever paid attention to forearms until now? How nice they seem, lithe and hard all at once, a vein or two raised under tan skin. I watch the hand nearest me disappear into the pocket of his pants, pulling out a pack of cigarettes. He offers me one.

"No, thank you."

He tosses his head, breathing in a long drag, then pushes a curl behind his ear. It doesn't catch, though, and when he smiles it brushes the top of his lashes.

"Where does your friend work?" I ask, petting Bruce, who has jumped onto the bench and rolled over so I can reach his belly.

"Cristiano and his sister own Club Fluid." He raises his arms in the air, gyrates with his hips. "It's where we like to dance. Do you like martinis? Silvia makes a good martini." He blows smoke out of his mouth when he says *martinis*.

"Vodka or gin?"

"Gin," he says, frowning. "Vodka is disgusting."

I prefer vodka, but don't say so.

He points at the terrier. "Bruce likes you."

There's that wry smile, as if he's in on some private joke at my expense. It's exasperating to be next to someone so young and confident. To feel your sore breasts, heavy like a pair of stones; to have your calves throb, your lower back ache. I want to say, *There are things I know that would wipe that smile off your face.*

Instead I look at my watch. "I have to meet Hannah."

He nods. "Piazza del Popolo."

I look at him but he's focusing on the dog now, pushing Bruce from the bench. "I'll walk with you," he says. He checks his phone. Starts to text someone. "Do you want a caffè?"

He takes me to one of the outdoor cafés in the park. It has a pretty green-and-white awning, potted flowers around wrought-iron tables and chairs. When we sit, a tired thin girl with dyed bright red hair comes over to take our order. Donato speaks beautiful, refined Italian. I can tell it isn't just me who thinks so, the girl has changed her stance, perked up a bit. He stops mid-sentence and switches to English. "Are you hungry?" he asks me.

I shake my head but I can tell when he starts up again that he's ordering food.

"Something light. We can eat again with Hannah."

Bruce has circled under his chair and lain down. The waitress brings us two espressos and a bottle of sparkling water. She smiles prettily at Donato now.

"How do you like Rome?" he asks when we're alone, tapping my guidebook, which I've set on the table.

Embarrassed, I slip it into my bag. "It's a bit overwhelming, to be honest. There's a lot to do."

"Don't worry, we will make sure you see everything."

"Do you mean you?"

"Sure," he says, tapping his breast. "But not Rick Steves's Rome, Donato's Rome. This is your first time in Italy?"

"It's my first trip to Europe. I haven't done much traveling."

He nods as if he understands. "Hannah says you take care of your mamma, and before that your *papà*."

I don't like the pity I hear in his voice. Caring for your parents as they age—that's what *good* children do. I clear my throat. "Hannah will want to know where I am."

"I already texted her." He grins. "She's going to meet us."

"Oh." I shift my weight in my chair. "Do you know Hannah's girlfriends too, I think their names are Trish and Tina?"

"Yes, and Gabriel and Leo and Silvia and Cristiano. You'll meet everyone."

"You hang out together?"

He takes out another cigarette and lights it. He reclines in his chair, shrugging his shoulders a little. "*Sì*, but Hannah is so much younger than the rest of us."

It suddenly occurs to me that he's trying hard to impress me. He wants me to like him, to think of him as an adult. A giddy laugh bubbles out of me.

"Donato," I say, delighted because I can tell he doesn't like being laughed at. "You are *both* very young."

The waitress with the dyed hair has brought out a caprese salad. She lingers for a moment, asking if she can get us anything else.

He's rude to her now, stubbing his cigarette out and swatting the air between them for her to go away. The waitress looks genuinely hurt, turning to clear a nearby table's empty prosecco glasses, shoulders slumped. I frown at him, but he doesn't seem to notice or care.

We eat in silence, slicing the underripe tomatoes, smearing them in the salty oil, the dripping, tender cheese. I watch an ant crawl along the table's edge. I can make out its dark body, the bulbous head, its tiny legs. Donato blows on it, hard enough to make it hunch down, turn, and go the other way.

"Not as young as her," he says, and squishes the ant with his finger.

When Hannah arrives, she sneaks up behind him. *Shhh*, she motions to me with a finger over her lips. "Doe-nat-oh!" she cries, messing up his hair.

"Basta," he says, pulling away from her.

She sticks her tongue out at him and drops into the empty chair beside me. "Oh, Auntie, I couldn't concentrate all day. I can't wait to show you everything. Have you two been having fun? Did you see the water clock in the park? That's my favorite."

"Cilla, just Cilla," I remind her. "We had an espresso and a salad. Donato offered to be my tour guide."

When the waitress brings the bill Donato and I both reach for it. "My treat," I say, snatching it from him and smiling. He pushes back from the table, the chair screeching.

Hannah shouts after him. He yells something over his shoulder.

"Where is he off to?"

"The bathroom, I guess," Hannah says, watching him walk away.

The waitress gives me a sour look when she takes my card. It's a look that says, *Your son, lady, is a spoiled brat.*

Hannah grabs my hand. "Are you guys getting along?"

"I don't think he's used to American women." I try to hide that I, too, am anxious that he like me.

"You have to get along," she says, frowning. She must have reapplied the bright blue eye shadow, because it's just as startling as it was this morning. She's added liquid black eyeliner that goes go up at the corners of each eye like tiny wings. I remember when Emily did her makeup like that—could Hannah have seen photos? How thin my sister was; barely an adult and going to parties in the Hollywood Hills, living with a boyfriend I didn't like. I can hear her saying it, *Stop mothering me, just stop!* If I were to trace back, chart the moments that shifted our relationship, those words would be somewhere at the beginning.

I squeeze Hannah's hand. "I'll be nice, I promise."

She wants to show me the Pincian Hill—*Il Pincio*, as Donato said when he returned from the bathroom. *It has the best views of the piazza.*

And it does. The park gives way, the city too, and there beneath us is a large piazza, an obelisk at the center. In the distance, Rome stretches out—all domed roofs, and aged stone and brick. Hannah wants me to take her picture with Donato and leaves me with the dog. She angles herself across him, her arm around his neck.

"Should I kiss her?" he asks me but doesn't wait for an answer. A quick peck on the lips, not brazen, not like the couple at the Forum, but Hannah is instantly a giggling mess, blushing in his arms. Tourists admiring the view have paused, costumed Roman gladiators stop hustling for photos—everyone watches them, this beautiful young couple, who look to be falling in love.

I'm tempted to delete the photo.

"Now a picture with *Zia* Cilla." Donato pushes Hannah toward me.

"No, no," I say.

But Hannah is delirious now. She is nearly hiccupping. "Pose, you two. Pose."

He puts his arm around my waist, mimics my rigid stance. He is smiling that mischievous smile again. I imagine those same tourists and costumed gladiators, who smiled and cooed at the sight of my niece and Donato, are watching us perplexed. *The way she is standing*, one of them must be thinking. *Not his mother, nor his sister. Maybe an old nanny . . .*

Donato says something in Italian to Hannah, which makes her dissolve into giggles again. "Relax," he says to me. "Relax."

He smells like whatever brand of cigarettes he smokes, which is unlike American cigarettes—all violet and spice. Both of his hands are on my hips now, those long knobby fingers applying pressure. *Relax.* He breathes near my ear. Liquid heat pools at the center of me, and I worry Hannah will see it in the photograph. Something mysterious in the smile, a forbidden pulsing behind those dark irises.

"One, two," Hannah counts. On three, he kisses me on the lips. It's quick and chaste, but I feel it everywhere.

"Friends?" he says to me as we walk down to the piazza, into the herds of people. "I will take you to my favorite bar if you let me buy the drinks."

I know I should say no—that I should take Hannah home, and in a few hours ring my mom to see how she is doing. "I'm very hot," I tell him, hoping this might be excuse enough.

"Negronis have a cooling effect," he says. He takes one hand, Hannah the other, and they steer me through the crowd.

Someone is playing the violin, there is an opera singer belting, and on the far side of the square, a dancing troupe blasting pop music from a boom box. The heat is oppressive, the sun blazing. But something about Donato's graceful charge, the ease with which he pulls us forward, flashing that carefree grin over his shoulder—I'm reminded again of that woman at the box office. He radiates it too: *Do not worry, Cilla.*

I lick my lips. "Okay, just one."

———

I forget where I am, why I'm in a twin bed instead of my California king. Where is the musty smell of old wood beams? The sound of surf crashing? And that acrid scent that Dad emitted as he grew sicker and sicker? You can still sometimes smell it in parts of our house when it's humid.

Instead I'm in a cramped rectangular room, swimming in sweat, my legs slick, my armpits, face, and scalp—hair twisted and matted. The A/C unit is rattling, but no cool air is coming out. I shut it off and reset it. I feel around until my eyes adjust, until I realize there is a moon, big and yellow. It is not actually that dark. I can make out the daisies in their turquoise vase, the dresser, the writing desk with my laptop setup. It is bright enough to see the far wall, to make out the photograph Hannah has taken and Paul has framed. The Ponte Sisto at night, buzzing silver and gold.

I can taste the gin still, the Campari and sweet vermouth. Donato had taken us to an art deco hotel, situated on a quiet street near the Piazza del Popolo. A favorite haunt of his. *Isn't it beautiful?* Hannah had said as we were seated in the courtyard, among blooming wisteria and potted ferns. Wrought iron and arched doorways. I had meant to drink only one cocktail, but it came and went so fast. I had barely cooled off. Only one more, I reasoned. Hannah wanted to order an Aperol spritz. *It isn't like America*, Donato said, sensing my hesitation. *Here we have bars in our cafés because there is no law that says this is when you are old enough to drink.* Besides, didn't Mom used to let me have Bellinis at Hannah's age? After I gave in, that was when we relaxed. Talking about the hotel's old Hollywood history—Douglas Fairbanks and Mary Pickford once stayed there, the menu had claimed. *I've worked at what used to be their studios*, I told them. *It's now called the Lot.* Laughing about the tourists in the piazza, the other patrons at the hotel, trying to guess whether they were Swedish or German or American by how they dressed.

It was flattering to see Hannah watch me, studying how I ordered the next round or sent something back if I wasn't satisfied. Donato watched too. Was this when I ordered a bottle of prosecco? Yes, because he had finally stopped trying to charm and embarrass me as if I were a granny. And because I liked the way he slouched into his chair, one arm outstretched over the back of mine, another button undone on his shirt so I could peek at the skin beneath, the smattering of springy dark hair at its center. He is so sinewy and long. Like a wild animal, like a well-exercised show horse.

His toothy grin said it, those flashing eyes said it too—*I know what you're thinking*. It humored him, gave him pleasure. And I didn't mind giving in, letting him know that I admired his profile. And Hannah seemed pleased to share his attention with me—the kind of satisfaction one gets from ordering correctly from the menu.

After the bottle of prosecco she wanted to hear stories about when her mother and I were young—about those long-ago parties.

Mom and Cilla were hanging out with famous writers and actors before they were old enough to walk, she bragged to Donato.

I told them how Mom's actress friends would do our makeup, how Dad's writer friends would read early drafts of their work to us at our bedtime. *I once corrected Guy's pronunciation of the word* façade. *I was seven.*

It was intoxicating to be in control of a room. I can't remember the last time I felt that way. When the waiter came with the bill I waved Donato off. This, I think, impressed Hannah most—I could tell that a woman denying Donato something does not happen often.

Hannah sat up taller, her smile became slightly haughty.

But then she was saying something about Guy.

It was scandalous, Cilla was only eighteen when they started dating, Guy was forty.

Thirty-three, I corrected her. *Almost thirty-four.* I had a headache from the prosecco. I could hear those bangles, see those delicate wrists. Eighteen is the official story. The one I told my parents, our friends. I've recited it so many times that it could almost be true. But I'm surprised Emily hadn't told Hannah the truth. She knew Guy and I had been together long before I was eighteen. She had been disgusted by it and told me so. I remember how I made her swear not to tell anyone, and how afterward she was cold to Guy. Mom and Dad asking, *What's wrong? Why won't you let him kiss you hello?*

Another thing Hannah had done, as we stood outside waiting for a cab, was she asked for a cigarette from Donato. *Don't smoke, Emily—I mean, Hannah.* It had been a reflex. Our mom preferred Nat Shermans, a habit my sister took up. It was something that had irked me at the time, as if Emily had started smoking just so they could have something else to exclude me from.

The cab ride to the apartment was a blur. I remember Hannah falling asleep between us, Rome looking ethereal in the dark. Somehow Donato managed to help Hannah up the stairs. She slept while he cooked for me. *I repay you for lunch*, he said, grinning that cocky grin. Paul was working late, I remember thinking. *Do not worry*.

I can still smell the pasta water and chili and roasted eggplant, it's no wonder Paul thought I had cooked when he finally got home. I did not correct him.

—

It's nearly dark. Cool air pumps from the air-conditioning, but I have the window open too. That dank scent has grown on me, and if I have to call my mother I want to be able to smell the city while doing it. I've spread out my postcard souvenirs across my lap: Trevi Fountain, Spanish Steps, St. Peter's Square, Circus Maximus. Donato has been an attentive tour guide. Each afternoon he is at the park, ready to show Hannah and me his city.

At the Colosseum he acted out famous gladiators who fought animals to the death. Hannah was enraptured. *When a gladiator died*, he said, gesturing with his hands, his arms, *attendants dressed as Charon, the ferryman, and carried his body away*.

That's so gruesome, Hannah had said, which made Donato laugh that openmouthed, throaty boy laugh.

There is great beauty in death, he said, putting his arm around her.

Or when he took us to Trajan's Market and we followed him through the halls and up steep stairs until we reached a balcony

53

overlooking the city center. Donato pointed out the Capitoline Hill, the forums of Caesar and Augustus, and the Altare della Patria, which he thought was ugly. *They destroyed a medieval neighborhood to build that*, he said, making a face.

Hannah practiced her Italian with him, thinking it hilarious that I couldn't understand a word.

I didn't come all this way to be a third wheel, I scolded her. She looked crestfallen, a little nervous as if I might leave and head back to the apartment—it reminded me so much of when Emily scolded her at that dinner, I regretted it immediately.

Oh, Cilla, she said, putting her head on my shoulder. *I'm sorry, please don't be mad. We'll speak in English, won't we, Donato?*

I carefully stack the postcards and put them on my bedside table, where my phone is blinking with another voice mail from my mom. *Gone five days and you've forgotten all about me. You've turned me into Dad, calling you to say how much I hate this place.*

Well, I do hate it. Call your mother back, for Christ's sake.

A warm balmy breeze blows in from the bedroom window; I breathe in that beguiling earthy smell. Musty, like a greenhouse or a cemetery. I pull the comforter up and put the earbuds in to call.

"She's eating lunch," the nurse says when I phone. "Let me see."

"Pricilla," comes Mom's raspy voice on the other end. "Pricilla, hello?"

"Hi, Mom, are they taking good care of you? How's lunch?"

"Never mind this hellhole. You must be having a grand time, you haven't called."

"I did, we just keep missing each other."

At first, she is bitter, withdrawn, but I know how to appease her. I ask about her doctor appointments, about physical therapy, until she launches into a story about a male orderly who she suspects is undocumented, and somehow this transitions into an episode with the Russian night nurse, who she's convinced keeps turning down her oxygen. *As if I don't know how much oxygen to give myself.* She needs someone to listen, so I do. But it's hard now, hearing her voice is like being hit with a weight.

I tune out just a little, just for self-preservation. I swipe through photos I took of Donato and Hannah at the Capitoline Hill. He is leaning against a banister, Hannah in front of him, his arms wrapped around her waist. They are posing on the stairs, monkeying around in the piazza. I want to tell my mom about when Donato wanted to photograph Hannah and me at the museum's café. The first one was of us together, then he posed us separately. Hannah with a sprig of rosemary, the city stretching out behind her. How pretty she looked, how well the light agreed with her. Emily had head shots done around Hannah's age, and I promised Hannah that I'd find them when I got home.

Now, Zia, Donato had said. And I played along, mostly because we had shared a split of prosecco with lunch, but also because I felt a lightness I hadn't felt in years.

Like this, Donato directed, angling my chin downward and pulling out my hair clip.

You look gorgeous like that! Hannah was in a fit of giggles.

It's no use, I said. *Photos of me do not turn out.*

Donato sent Hannah to ask for another split of prosecco.

It's that cardigan, he said after she'd gone. *It is for an old lady. Take it off.*

I hesitated; he had that teasing look about him again. But

that heat at the center tempted me. We are playing a game, I told myself.

Bellissimo. Bellissimo. He took the photo.

I hurried to put the cardigan back on before my niece returned.

Let me see, I said.

He held his phone to his chest. *For my eyes only.* He would not even show Hannah.

"Mom," I interrupt. "I'm sending out postcards tomorrow. Do you want one with religious images, or a fountain?"

The sounds of the nursing home invade my room.

"I'd rather have a picture of my granddaughter. You haven't sent me one. How is she? How's Paul?"

I get up to close the window, the blanket wrapped around me. "He's been very welcoming. He's giving me a tour of the university tomorrow."

"Give him my love. And Hannah? Does she look like Emily?"

"Very much so." There is an ache right behind my eye. I open the window again.

"She's been very sweet," I manage to add. "I think it's good that I came."

My mom is silent. There is only the oxygen concentrator's raspy beating. A death rattle sounds similar. That last haggard breath Dad took, big and gasping. Like a rake over gravel.

"I'll text your iPad a picture after we hang up."

"Your poor sister," she starts.

"Don't upset yourself," but I can tell she's already crying. "Did the psychiatrist ever prescribe you something to help you sleep?"

She isn't listening, though; I hear her ask the nurse for a box of tissues.

I'm remembering now that Hannah had said something to Donato this afternoon, while we were trying on clothes at an expensive shop near the Piazza di Spagna, on the crowded Via Condotti. The saleswoman knew Donato well, taking his hands in hers. She picked out outfits for each of us to try on, and I remember being in one of the fitting rooms, deciding if a silk crepe dress could make me look sultry or not, when I heard Hannah tell Donato, *My mom and Cilla did not get along.*

How much could a child know? She was so young during those first few incidents, and then there was a period where we just didn't see each other. Cards and presents were mailed, always on time. There were a handful of get-togethers for Mom's birthday, Emily and I were civil to each other by then. Strangers, sure. But perfectly civil.

What had Emily said to Hannah about me, about Guy, about our dad's final days?

I peered out from the fitting room, and saw Donato in a flashy two-piece jacquard suit, Hannah modeling a slim-fit dress in fuchsia hibiscus print. She looked so much like Emily, not only her facial features, but how she unwittingly awed the room. The saleswoman who had been so partial to Donato was now doting on her. *Such a lovely figure,* she said.

"Mom, Emily's at peace," I try. I can hear her weeping now.

I find a pack of cigarettes on the desk. I hid them a few nights ago just as Paul got home. They are Donato's.

Quietly, quietly, I open the desk drawers, moving papers and Post-its, stamps and knickknacks. Finally, I find a box of matches.

"I miss her so much," she says, sniffling a little.

"I know, Mom. Eat the rest of your lunch and I'll call again soon."

She sounds tired now. "Don't forget to text me that photo."

"I promise," I tell her.

We hang up and I slide a cigarette out, bringing it to my nose. It smells just like him. I fix the filter between my lips, tonguing it a little, just so I know what it tastes like. Starchy, slightly floral. The match makes a satisfying sound, a loud scratch. I inhale deeply. It tastes delicious. I get light-headed, but I don't put it out. I let it burn, like incense.

———

The university isn't far, but I have to pass the train station, which is large, industrial, and packed with people. It's the kind of crowd that wouldn't give a second thought if I were pushed into traffic. And most of them would do the pushing—businessmen with roll bags, students with huge lumbering backpacks, families trying to stay together. They've all got places to be and I'm in the way.

When I cross the street, a hustler follows. He's hawking jewelry, water bottles, miniature electric fans. He seems to know I'm American and speaks English.

"Signora, let me give this to you, it's free—gratis, gratis. A gift because you are so beautiful. *Bella, bella.*" But then he must second-guess himself, because he switches to French, breaking into song, *"Parole, parole, parole, Je t'en prie, Parole, parole, parole, Je te jure."* He covers his heart as if struck by Cupid's arrow. I give in and buy a bracelet. I buy two, one for Hannah and one for Donato.

I got my period this morning, but to describe it that way seems wrong. More like dried seeds, crushed together to make a stain. Not like the periods of my youth, when the bleeding was so heavy I sometimes napped in the nurse's office during school.

This morning I waited in bed, while Paul, trying to be quiet, urged Hannah, *Get a move on.* Drawers in the bathroom opening and closing, then Hannah hissing back, *Where's my fucking hairbrush?* When they finally left I could only find super tampons.

But of course that's what I would find. She's fifteen years old, for God's sake, her womb probably gushes blood and mucosal tissue.

As I turn onto Via del Castro Pretorio, a sense of calm returns. The street is lined with broadleaf trees, dappling the road and sidewalk cafés, the buildings are faded gold and orange. Lampposts decorate the sidewalk, mopeds are parked outside busy shops. I try to remind myself that these buildings don't just look Renaissance, they probably *are* Renaissance, or at least Renaissance revival. But it's no use, it still doesn't feel real. A backdrop for a big-budget thriller, or an independent melodrama, maybe. Hollywood has ruined me. I've lived in an imitation world my whole life.

The walk is longer than I thought it would be. It's early, but the humidity is already thick. I consider flagging down a cab, but they aren't lined up and waiting like they were outside the tourist spots. Several race by, I can't tell if they're in service. The trees grow thinner, the sidewalk more worn and cracked. There is graffiti and trash; the assaulting stench of human feces, made sharper by the heat. Even this feels scripted. The ancient city turned modern and ugly.

At the entrance of the school, I text Paul and try to adjust the tampon string in my underwear without the heavily armed guards noticing. Itchy and so uncomfortable. I can't remember the last time I used a tampon, let alone a super tampon. It's probably stuck in there for life.

"Cilla, ciao!" Paul says, coming out to fetch me. He kisses my cheek.

"Oh, Paul, I'm exhausted," I tell him. "I could fall asleep right here."

"You didn't walk, did you? Christ, Cilla, that's nearly three miles and the last bit is a pretty rough neighborhood." He slips my purse from my shoulder and takes my arm.

"You must be starving. We can eat with Marie and Tonio first." He leads me past the guards, who laugh when Paul says something to them in Italian.

"Carabinieri," he says to me. "Every university has them now. The churches and museums and the tourist sites—Rome is always *allerta*."

"Did something happen?"

He sighs. "This is a city that lives with anxiety," he says. "So much has happened here. Romans have seen the best of human-kind, but also the worst."

Tonio is waiting for us in the cafeteria, looking very much like the studious professor in a three-piece suit. From afar I can tell he once had the same slim, long-limbed build as Donato. A pang, brief but sharp: What is he doing right now? I picture that easy breezy smile, and blush stupidly when Tonio takes my hand and kisses my cheek.

"Marie will be late," he tells us.

Lunch is disappointing. The cafeteria is lackluster, more like an Internet café than a proper restaurant. Even with the fans the air feels dormant. Flies lumber over congealed pizza, there is hardly any green in the salad. But Paul and Tonio don't seem to mind. They fork piles of pesto linguine into their talking mouths. Paul uses a roll to wipe the remaining sauce from his plate. The beer is good and cold, though.

"The campus is not beautiful," Tonio apologizes. "Many of the buildings were built by the Fascists."

"Ignore him," Paul says. "He's worked here for thirty years."

"It feels much longer."

"Is this where Donato will go?" It feels good to say his name out loud, so I say it again. "*Donato* mentioned he was taking a year off first, but afterward will he come here?"

Tonio frowns, shaking his head. "He will go to the university when he is done with *scuola superiore*." He launches into Italian then, and Paul listens closely.

I can't shake the feeling of being an accessory. I'm reminded of when Emily and I were little, before our parents left us at home with just the housekeeper—back when we had a housekeeper and the house was new and money wasn't tight. Sometimes we accompanied them to a premiere. Mom spent hours getting us ready. There were shopping trips to Bullock's and Bloomingdale's—she'd have the same person who did her hair and makeup do ours. How sweet the four of us looked in those early photos. A brief happy period, but then Mom's career took a turn, and for almost a decade she did not work. Only threw parties at the house. She had a brief resurgence in the '90s, cast in another soap. It meant part of the year she was alone in New York, but it also meant she was photographed again. This time with only Emily—in *TV Guide* and *People*, photographed in matching Jenny Packham. "Mother and Daughter Look-alikes," the headline read. Which was fine, because I had Guy by then. *Someone needs to take care of you . . .*

I almost breathe a sigh of relief when I see Marie. She waves to us from the cafeteria entrance. Paul waves back, motioning for her to come over. But then they are all about work. I try to keep up, to feign interest, but the three of them with their books and papers spread out on the cafeteria table; their little intimacies—sharing a coffee, ordering for one another, never arguing over who will pay a bill, how deep and seamless their conversations are—there isn't room for anyone else.

Donato is probably already at the park with Bruce. I wonder how quickly I can get away. I'm thinking about last night, when we were at a hotel bar and the DJ started to play music. Donato asked Hannah to dance—how radiant the two of them looked. And how she erupted into laughter when he tried to dance with me. *No, no, not me.* I do not dance. *Ahhh*, he said, grabbing at his heart exactly like the street hustler had grabbed at his. Then he whisked Hannah up again. The look she gave me from his arms—she was reveling in it.

I realize Marie is talking to me. "Have we worn you out completely?"

She's in a printed dress, cinched at her waist and long, covering her short legs. A voluptuous woman. With her hat perched slightly at an angle, her round pink cheeks and large dark eyes, she looks like a cherub come to life. I'm suddenly more aware of my small breasts; of how broad and tall I am in comparison. *My bear*, my dad used to call me. Emily was always his *little lamb*.

"No, not at all. It's the heat and I can't shake the jet lag, I keep waking up early," I lie. "My mind is mush."

She's sympathetic, patting my arm. "Tomorrow I have a treat planned for us."

After espressos we part, and Paul takes me to see the university's sculpture collection.

"They're only plaster casts of more famous works," he says, carrying my purse for me. "But it's a grand collection nonetheless."

On the way he recites the history of not just the school, but various neighborhoods in Rome. He wants me to see the botanical gardens in Trastevere, the Appian Way outside the city center. "There's not enough time," he laments. I don't tell him that Donato has already taken me to the botanical gardens, that I have pictures of him in front of the greenhouse in a sea of orchids.

He clears his throat when he catches me glancing at my phone. We've stopped to admire a modest statue of a man in a cowl. "The politician Cola di Rienzo," he gestures. "He was murdered by an angry mob."

"That's terrible," I say. My phone vibrates. A text from Hannah.

—*I got out early.*

"Is that Hannah?" he asks anxiously. "How is she doing? She's become such a stranger to me. When she was little, she'd cry when I'd leave for work."

My phone vibrates again.

—*Meet us at Silvia's!*

There's an address. I feel a stab of jealousy, and miss what Paul is saying. He's sitting down on a bench, running a hand over his face.

"I think about how you and Emily at least had each other—"

"Having a sibling isn't always a blessing. And she's fifteen, Paul." I sit beside him. "By then Emily and I were different people—she was already picking up surfers on the beach."

I remember that day easily because I think of it often. Emily, flipping her hair and lowering her lashes, beaming at whatever the surfers said. I tried to get her to go home with me—she was maybe fourteen, and I could see gray in the surfers' chest hair. One of them called me a prude, and I remember Emily laughing. It was such an affected laugh, so docile and unlike her, that I shielded my eyes against the glare, and tried to make her out. There she was in her teal bikini, my little sister, open-mouthed, laughing at me. *Prude*, she repeated. *If you only knew.* I shoved her hard enough that she fell into the surf. She had a bruise on her thigh for the rest of that summer.

"I used to wish I had a brother or sister," Paul is saying.

"You do." I nudge him, and he chuckles.

"Em used to tell me how you watched out for her when you two were little." He looks at me. "What happened? You were close when she was pregnant with Hannah. Was it because we moved?"

I don't want to talk about this. It's as if the air has changed suddenly, I swear I can smell the Pacific, her banana-perfumed sunscreen. "San Clemente isn't that far," I mumble, and get up from the bench.

He follows, but a group of students have entered the gallery, their footsteps echoing off the marble walls. One of them stops. *Professore.*

Another text from Hannah.

—*Are you on your way?*

I text back, *I'll be right there.* I add a taxi emoji and then delete it at the last minute.

"I have to meet Hannah," I tell him. "Thanks for the tour."

I leave, Paul looking after me. I can't help it. *Sisters leave wounds*, I wanted to tell him. Minor betrayals, petty grievances—over time, they add up and create an impassable distance. *Hannah should consider herself lucky.*

I give the cabdriver the address Hannah texted, and ask him to turn up the air conditioner. He doesn't understand, though, and the leather seat is hot from the sun. My thighs will stick when I get out. "A/C," I repeat. The driver nods but doesn't do anything.

I pull up my e-mail on my phone. The roofer has come through with an estimate, and the gardener has sent a landscape quote. I start to reply, but then stop. I look out at Rome, let myself be dazzled by its metallic sheen, the sagging sycamores over the Tiber, how their branches sway and broad leaves rustle in the warm, lively breeze. I can feel myself slipping into it, or maybe it's slipping into me.

I take a compact out of my purse. I don't wear more than mascara, but when I searched Hannah's bathroom I found a makeup bag packed with lipsticks. I took a tinted lip balm that smelled like artificial strawberries. My niece hasn't noticed; they're probably all stolen anyway.

I spread it across my lips, smacking them together. This the cabdriver understands. He smiles at me in the rearview mirror.

———

Time is different in Rome. Maybe it's the light, which is languid and delicate. The blue afternoon bleeds into twilight like a watercolor, and I realize we've been up on Silvia's terrace drinking aperitifs for nearly five hours. Donato's friends in crisp suit jackets, hair slicked back, plumes of smoke climbing into the now golden sky. Hannah and her girlfriends, their boisterous chatter mixing with the city noises below: a car horn, a motorcycle, a police siren, sandals clack-clacking on the narrow cobblestone streets.

My niece had been the one to open the door. She tried her best to be nonchalant. *Auntie*, she cried. But I knew that look. Emily had the same expression when I caught her smoking a joint with the neighbor. *Guilty*.

I almost didn't come inside, I almost demanded Hannah leave, but then Silvia appeared, and I was thrown off. She was older than I expected, older than Donato, with large green eyes and a pretty pout. I could smell her perfume, something expensive, a fragrance that reminded me of home. She smelled like magnolias and the sea.

The two of them ushered me up to the terrace, which felt

ten degrees cooler than the rest of the city. Potted palms and geraniums and impatiens shaded the patio furniture, a breeze rustling their leaves. Powder-blue parakeets, each named after a Roman deity, chirped in a large gilded birdcage.

Diana, Diana, Silvia cooed to one of them, showing me how to feed the tiny bird by hand.

Their friends were waiting on the terrace; one had already made me a drink. Cristiano, Silvia's brother, moved so I could take his seat. The two auburn-haired British sisters, Trish and Tina, wanted to show me their head shots. *Cilla knows all the right people*, my niece told them. What I'm saying is, it was easy to be seduced.

"Do you want another?" Hannah is asking. I feel a wave of tenderness looking at her. The light is glossy and bright, strangely hypnotic.

I take her hand. "Maybe one more."

"Did you like how I made it last time? More prosecco?"

"It was perfect."

It's hard to say no to her. Especially when she looks so eager for my approval. I remember when Emily used to look at me like that.

You look so much like your mother—too late, she's already gotten up. I wish now I hadn't sent her away. I want to tell her about Emily's pregnancy. I want to explain how we had grown apart. *Your mother pushed me away.* But then, when she got pregnant, she wanted my help with everything. What colors should the baby's room be? Which furniture should she buy? She wanted help quitting smoking, a walking partner in the mornings, someone to throw her a baby shower. I decorated our mom's courtyard with mermaids and leis, and invited twenty of her girlfriends.

It's such an honor to be someone's mommy, I remember one of them saying over cake. How self-righteous they were, pitying glances thrown in my direction. Well, I can think of other proverbs. *A mother is never free*, our mom used to say.

Silvia lets out a laugh at something Donato has said. She's moved so she can stretch her tan legs across him. I'm watching him massage her feet.

"Did Donato show you Santa Maria del Popolo?" she's asking me. "It has my favorite Caravaggio."

Donato says something in Italian, which makes her laugh again.

"It's where Nero's ghost lives," one of the British sisters says to me. "Do you know Nero?"

I remember Donato pointing out a domineering building in the piazza. But I don't remember him telling us about any ghosts.

Cristiano is rolling a joint on his lap. "*Omicida.*" He lights it.

"He dipped Christians in oil," another one of them is saying as they pass the joint around.

"And set them on fire to light his garden at night."

"He killed his mother."

The smoke is very strong, the air suddenly stagnant.

"How do you live with so many reminders of death everywhere?" I ask. The breeze returns and I shiver.

"It reminds us to live well," Donato says, puffing on the joint. "That this life is short. You have to take what you want."

I have not thought about my wants in so long that the flood of them makes me light-headed. A drip-irrigation system for the garden, my own Tiffany stud earrings so I don't have to always be borrowing Mom's, one of those mid-century modern houses in Benedict Canyon, a buzzy TV show—Guy.

"*Sii prudente.*" Silvia clicks her tongue. "Want is insatiable. Even the gods were never satisfied."

Donato makes a dismissive motion with his hand. She gets up to play with her parakeets, Bruce barking at her heels. The others are talking about an upcoming trip to the Aeolian Islands. Donato is sitting beside me now. His eyes have darkened, that mischievous smile playing on his lips.

"You smell like strawberries," he says. He offers me the joint. "You want to try?"

A little thrill shoots through me.

That square chin and aquiline nose—that dark untamed hair. He must have been a beautiful baby. I can picture it perfectly: baby Donato is fussy, with latching difficulties. Child Donato scrapes his knee riding a bicycle, bumps his head on the playground, makes a mess in the kitchen with the juice. I can imagine scolding him, or cleaning his bleeding knee, or kissing the hurt forehead. For a brief moment, I feel a pull in my womb, a ferocious sting in my nipples.

I take a drag on the joint and exhale just as Hannah comes out with the aperitifs.

"Aunt Cilla!" she cries. "I can't believe Donato got you to smoke pot!"

Her amusement embarrasses me and I try to sit up taller, straighten my blouse and slacks. But twilight is finally waning, evening is almost here, and my eyes are having a hard time adjusting to the change in light.

"I'm hungry," comes Donato's voice, and then Hannah has switched places with him, wiggling in close.

"Sorry it took me so long, Papa called. I said we were seeing a movie."

Her voice has given me a headache. I can feel the heat of her body through our clothes. It's reminded me of just after Hannah was born, of those late-night phone calls where my sister cried and told me that she wished she had terminated the pregnancy. *I don't know why I wanted this.* I didn't know what to say. *It'll be all right. Women have babies all the time.*

I ask Hannah to get me water but Donato volunteers.

"Silvia," he calls out. "Come downstairs with me."

I feel every cell bristle. Of course, they are together, and why should that matter to me anyway?

Hannah puts her head on my shoulder. "Do you think Silvia is very pretty?"

Tiny lights strung across the terrace turn on and I can see her watery eyes. Below I hear Donato's laugh.

"She's a lot older than him," I say.

"Only by five years."

Her body starts to shake, tears fall on my shoulder. "Hush," I tell her. "Hush." Instinctively I look around to see if any of their friends are watching.

"Come on." I pull her up from the settee. "Call us a ride, and I'll get your backpack. We can pick up a pizza on the way home."

I wipe the smeared mascara from under her eyes and point her toward the stairs. I say goodbye to her friends, making up an excuse that Paul wants us home. *He's made dinner.* I can tell Donato doesn't believe this, but he doesn't say so. When he kisses my cheek, I cannot help it, I press him against me. He feels broader than I thought he would, and that liquid fire at the center of me rejoices.

In the cab Hannah gives in. She is bawling.

"I miss Mom," she chokes out. "I miss her so much."

Letting her drink was probably a bad idea, but isn't she old enough to know her limit? Or at least learn what it is? I knew not to drink a third Bellini at fifteen, or if Guy offered to make me a screwdriver, to drink it slowly because he always made them very strong. I stroke the spot between the shoulder blades that used to comfort Emily. More like her mother then. Sensitive. Delicate. Upset because our parents missed another recital; a boy she liked didn't return her affection; a wave knocked her into the sand. "I know, sweetheart," I say. "It'll be okay."

She sniffs. "Will you run your hands through my hair? Mom used to do it whenever I was upset."

Her hair is finer than Emily's, which had been coarse from flat-ironing and blow-drying.

Shhh, it'll be all right. Our mom doing something like this when we were small. It only happened a handful of times. After a shower, or bath. We'd sit obediently in front of her, and even though there would be knots, we never squirmed, never complained. At that age we still wanted so badly to be near her that anything, no matter how painful, was worth it.

My eyes well up. I'm not used to smoking weed. The darkness outside the cab feels claustrophobic. Every pothole dangerous.

I remember a statue Paul showed me this afternoon at the university: the she-wolf of Rome. Romulus and Remus at her teats. I can picture it, the engorged breasts, the wolf's nipples hanging low—the two small children, mouths opened, suspended in that moment before suckling.

She bares her teeth as she turns toward us in fear, Paul had said, describing the wolf's expression.

Fear of what exactly? Which part of motherhood scared her most?

———

Emily and I are lying out on towels. She is so thin, I can make out every rib, the sternum, the knobby bulges of her shoulders. Her hair is golden and thick, though, which is how I know I'm dreaming. It was so brittle toward the end. I want to lie here even though I'm not sure if beside me Emily is alive or dead. When a coyote is hit on Pacific Coast Highway, the carcass will decay for weeks until all that's left is bones and fur. I can wait, I'm willing to wait. The sun is warm, and maybe if we lie here long enough the tide will rise and the current will drag us out, maybe the sea will accept us back into it.

My phone vibrates and drops onto the floor, waking me. I've fallen asleep in my clothes. It's not yet eleven. I have a voice mail from Guy. It's startling to hear his voice, casual and familiar, telling me that Mom is doing well, the production too. He doesn't ask me to call, but I don't want to be alone, thinking of that hideous death.

How could I have known it would be quick? Paul had only called a few weeks earlier to say Emily was coming home from the hospital, that hospice had been arranged. I brought a tuna casserole, without peas, which was how Emily liked it when she was little. But she was already in a drug-induced sleep by then. Paul and the caregivers administering liquid morphine every two hours. *So thin*, I remember saying to Paul, who looked at me bewildered. *She's been thin for months*, he said. They asked if I wanted to rub lotion into her hands, put a warm washcloth on her face. *She knows you're here*, someone said. I did not want to see her die. I did not want to touch her body. Downstairs I microwaved the casserole and sat and ate it with Hannah while we watched cartoons.

Guy doesn't answer the first time, so I call again. A third time.

"Pricilla, what time is it there?" I can hear car horns; a radio being turned down. I imagine he's on a freeway stuck in traffic and I feel a twinge of homesickness.

"Not that late." I open the bedroom window. Below, the

courtyard is in shadow, the lemon tree sagging from the hot afternoon. "I wanted to know how the house is, you didn't say in your message. Have you gone by?"

He starts to rattle off about watering the houseplants, the garden, collecting the mail—I let him talk, comforted by his voice.

I think of dancing for him, all those years ago. *Slowly, slowly.* That look on his face, maybe that's when I learned to recognize lust. If not, then it was when he tucked that flower in my dress at my birthday party, his fingers cool against my breasts. How he licked his lips a little. *His* want, I learned. But what about my own? I wanted Guy, or maybe I needed him to want me. Another line blurred, but that's how it is for women. Want, need—one and the same, expanding or contracting to fit the scene.

"Come on! Move it!" Guy curses. I hear him slap his steering wheel in frustration. "Sorry, babe, it rained last night and everyone in LA has lost their goddamn minds."

Emily had been the only one home when we first had sex. I remember hearing her shouting from the deck. *Cilla? Cilla?* But I was down on the beach—Guy's fingers pulling at my underwear, struggling with a condom. I barely had to do anything at all. *Cilla, where are you?* My sister's voice, carried by the wind.

"I haven't been feeling very well," I blurt out.

"What's wrong, flu? Those tourist sites are cesspools."

His concern is real, but his tenderness only makes me sadder because it isn't the kind that's between two lovers. Our relationship changed sometime after Dad got sick, or maybe right before. I was so busy with medications and doctor appointments and physical therapy and grocery shopping and cooking that I missed when it happened. A gradual shift, like the changing of a tide.

"I've been having hot flashes," I tell him. "And headaches, and I've been so tired."

He clears his throat. I think I can hear his engine shifting gears. "It's probably about that time, isn't it?"

Now I really want to cry. "I'm only forty-three."

"Have you seen a doctor?" he asks. He must cover the phone, because I hear him talking but can't make out the words.

"Is someone in the car with you?"

"No, I'm alone," he says, but I know he's lying. Trudy is probably sitting right beside him. I don't know why I thought it would be otherwise.

A few months ago he asked me to dinner. He sent a PA to pick me up, something he hadn't done in decades—and then at the film location there was Guy, yelling at the gaffers and grips. I felt sixteen again. The camera crew patiently waiting for him to be satisfied; soon he'd hand the production over to the assistant director and we'd speed off in his convertible. I felt that old reverence for him, a deep, complicated love. When we did leave the set, he took the bends in the canyon at full speed as if we were both young. I remember him putting his arm around me because I had been cold, and how it felt to be snuggled up to him once more, how when his lips brushed my hair I became giddy.

And then, there was Trudy waiting for us at the valet.
You didn't tell me she was meeting us.

He smiled slyly. *Would you have come?* He looked so much like a naughty, misbehaving child that I wanted to slap him.

Over dinner I realized he didn't merely want me to like her, he wanted my approval. How could I give him that? I watched her look around the room while Guy talked, smiling at the bartender, arranging herself so the tables nearby had more to look at. Or when she sulked because she ordered the wrong drink.

I always get manhattans and cosmos confused! Even her voice was childish and insincere. I wanted to spit in her drink and scream at Guy, *Why am I not enough?*

"It's an inferno here," Guy says, changing the subject. "We've had a hell of a time keeping the studio air-conditioned. And one of the trailers broke. I'm not using Quixote next time, remind me of that. I think it'll push us over budget. We need another investor."

"Don't you have a secretary to tell this to? Or an executive producer?"

"Not as good as you." I can tell he's smiling. "I've got another call coming in, but can I send you some figures later? I need a second pair of eyes."

I tell him yes, of course.

That's my girl.

I hang up. I can feel the weight of his presence, as if he were in the room. I should shower, go to bed, but I don't feel tired. I find where I've hidden Donato's cigarettes and light one. The night air is warm, the city calm. A pair of spotlights search the sky. I picture Trudy and Guy, driving together, his arm around her. How cruel it is, to get old. To be able to survey a life and see how it's played out.

Across the courtyard, I hear a window slide open. I freeze, cigarette in midair. A light switches on, and there is Donato, in just a towel. It is shocking to see him, like a flashlight shined directly into my pupils. I can feel them dilate, I can feel my whole body swell and open.

He sees me and tilts his head, running his hands through his hair. He smiles that knowing, teasing smile. I can see his biceps flexing, the muscles in his chest and stomach—the faint ones on his sides that come down to a point where his towel is tied.

Something is happening, I don't think I could stop it even if I wanted to. I've slipped my blouse off, unclasping the hooks of my bra. I watch Donato lean forward, he isn't smiling anymore. He has that look, the one I haven't seen on a man in a long time. I suck on the end of that cigarette and blow out toward him, imagining the smoke will travel the length between us. Then I shut the window and close the curtain.

My whole body is shaking. I start to laugh but then remember everyone is sleeping. I have to cover my face with a pillow.

———

"Isn't it beautiful?" Paul has stopped walking to point out another crumbling ruin. This one, he tells Hannah and me, used to be a basilica. Workers are erecting a stage in the remaining façade, electrical equipment already hangs from its arches. Paul calls to them in Italian and they stop to chat.

I lean against a wall, under the shade of bougainvillea, and fan myself with a brochure he got for me at an information center. He roused us early this morning. *Cilla needs to walk in the footsteps of the Romans*, he argued. Hannah refused to go until Paul promised to drop us off afterward at the day spa. *We'll have earned it*, Hannah said under her breath. I assumed she meant because Paul can be long-winded and didactic, not that we'd be navigating a lopsided, shadeless road for miles.

Hannah plunks down beside me. "It is *so* hot."

"They're setting up for a concert," Paul says to us. "We should come back tonight."

My niece looks incredulous. "But it's Saturday! Donato and I wanted to take Cilla to Club Fluid."

Paul tries to hide a frown. My poor brother-in-law has been trying to keep us entertained with stories of aqueducts and emperors, wealthy patricians and martyrs. But Hannah is fifteen, and all I can think of is that look on Donato's face. How when he leaned forward, his hands gripped the windowsill. My stomach does a little flip every time and I want to cackle.

We take a break at a roadside café that has a view of the surrounding fields. A brisk dry wind picks up, pulling at the few ragged pines. Twice it knocks over our umbrella, and the owner comes out to ask if we want to move inside.

"Cities of death," Paul says, stirring sugar into his caffè. "That's what Romans called the catacombs. The Christians called it a *coemeterium*, a place of rest."

Hannah rolls her eyes, pushing her spoon around in her melting gelato.

"*Horror ubique animos simul ipsa silentia terrent*," Paul recites.

"What does that mean?" I've ordered a sparkling water, which is flat but ice cold.

The wind outside blows a pair of bikes over. The owner goes out to pick them up, the waitress helping him.

"It's from the *Aeneid*. A student in the fourth century quoted it when he saw the catacombs for the first time. *Everywhere horror seizes the soul, and the very silence is dreadful.*"

"Ugh! Papa, you are so morbid," Hannah cries, dropping her spoon onto the table.

Paul looks hurt. "Maybe I'm not explaining it right."

When we reach the catacombs Hannah and I slip out of our sandals to cool our feet in a fountain. She laughs when I splash her. But as our tour group readies for the descent, she becomes withdrawn. I notice she's biting her nails. *Is something the matter?* But she shrugs me off.

A cold air emits from the mouth of the entrance. I hear a child from another family start to cry. "Shh, shh," the mother says. The light getting darker and darker, the temperature dropping.

"You do not want to be last," the guide jokes when we've reached the first underground level. "Two days it will take for me to find you."

Laughter echoes in the long black corridors. There are carved-out holes in the walls where bodies once rested.

"The bones," Paul whispers to me, "have been moved. They're two levels below us now. More than half a million of them."

It's dimly lit but I can make out Hannah on the other end of the room, her arms wrapped around herself.

"Paul, do you think this is a little much for Hannah?"

The tour group has stopped to admire a relief of the Virgin Mary, the blue of her dress still vibrant.

"Emily talked to her about death," Paul says. "To try to prepare her."

"She was barely twelve." I'm surprised by how upset I sound.

"No, I mean before her diagnosis."

It takes me a moment to realize what incident he's referring to, but then I can hear my sister and me screaming at each other in the nursing home parking lot.

We've read books on dying, Emily shouted. *She understands what's happening.*

She's four, I yelled back. *Dad is dying in there—he's barely conscious. This is not a fucking teachable moment.*

I refused to let them go in. Hannah started to cry—frightened, I'm sure, by our screaming, how red and sweaty my face had become. And I used those tears to get Mom on my side. *See?* I cried. *She shouldn't be here, she's too young.* I knew as Emily sped off that she would not return. In her mind, I had prevented her from saying goodbye to her father. Which, in a way, I had.

I fight an urge to describe to Paul how labored my dad's

breathing had been at the end. *It haunts me still*, I want to tell him.

"Hannah didn't need to see her grandfather like that," I say instead. "It would have scarred her for life."

"I'm sure you're right."

The tour group moves on to the next crypt. This one has a statue of a woman lying on her side, head turned toward the floor. Fake oil lamps flicker on either side of it.

"St. Cecilia," the guide says. "This is how the body was found when it was exhumed. They tried three times with the axe." He makes slashing motions to his neck. "But they could not cut through."

There is a flurry of photography.

"They left her here like that?" I ask.

"*Sì*," the tour guide says. "To die alone."

I can see Dad, the version of him in death. It happened a few days after Emily and Hannah's failed visit. His mouth slack on one side, his cheeks gaunt. I went with Mom to pick out the coffin. Polished mahogany finish, plush cream interior. I read over the contract for her, made sure the mortuary had my cell number. I ordered catering and sent out e-mails and fielded phone calls. When Emily texted, I replied that I had it under control. *Of course you do*, she messaged back. How complicated our relationship had become—to start out like two tiny vines and end up a rat's nest of branches and thorns. We barely spoke during the service.

"Thank God," Hannah says, climbing the stairs out of the catacombs two at a time. "I thought that tour would never end."

The heat hits us before we've made it to the top, the cicadas buzzing like electric saws.

Paul wants to stop in the gift shop with the rest of the tourists. Junk, cheap religious trinkets. Gold-plated pendants, devotional cards and pens emblazoned with an image of the Pope. I talk him out of buying me a souvenir book. "Don't you want to get something for Guy?" he asks, flipping through it so I can see the catacombs once more. "No, thank you," I say. On the cab ride back into the city, I try to replay that image of Donato in his window.

"What did you think?" Paul interrupts me.

"Of the catacombs?"

He motions to the scenery passing by. Hannah has fallen asleep on my shoulder. "The whole thing."

"It's amazing, unreal."

"That's truer than you realize. Men on their Grand Tour expected to see the Rome of the Neoclassical period—the stuff of Piranesi, and James Barry, Jacques-Louis David. Those cypresses and stone pines." He points. "They were planted to add to the evocativeness. You can't tell the real Rome from the fantasy."

A set after all, at least partially. I'm oddly comforted by this, a familiar artificiality. I look out my window, the sun is beating hard against the glass. Unmarked slabs, ruins, more ruins, arid fields. It feels urgent that I remember last night. I close my eyes. His bedroom light turns on—and for a moment his body is in silhouette. Then sleek, hard lines. I can hear my bra unclasping. How serious his expression was, and those large hands gripping the windowsill. I replay it over and over—afraid, because already the memory feels insufficient.

Marie's treat is an afternoon at a day spa, a hammam, in the Jewish Ghetto. When Paul drops Hannah and me off after the catacombs, she and a girlfriend are already waiting for us.

"We were at school together," Marie explains to me. "And our sons are in school together. We are old friends."

"You know Donato?" I ask.

"She doesn't speak very good English," Marie says. The front desk attendant sells me flip-flops and a pair of gloves. Hannah and Marie and Marie's friend have brought their own. In the locker room there is classical music playing and it's warm, warmer than it was outside.

"I love humidity as long as I'm naked," Hannah says, pulling off her shorts and shoving them into a locker.

"Was it a very long tour?" Marie asks. She helps her friend unhook her bra.

"Ugh, endless."

They slip out of their clothes without a whiff of self-consciousness, as if they've been naked around each other a hundred times before.

"Do you need help?" Marie offers, because I'm not as quick to undress as them. I realize I'm wearing the same bra from last night, when I exposed myself to her son.

"No, no, I'm fine," I say, waving her away.

They've wrapped themselves in towels, and after I've done the same, we file through the far door and continue down a set of stairs, where it's darker and warmer. We emerge in what looks like an ancient underground church. The walls are concave brick, there is incense burning, frankincense and amber. And another, mustier smell, similar to the catacombs, to Rome after a rain shower. Candles give the illusion of a place for pagan worship. Everywhere are naked women. Short, tall, dark, white—every color in between.

Some are old, much older than me, their breasts sagging

painfully, their areolas enormous, their nipples pinched and shriveled.

I watch Marie and her friend lie on their towels. I don't think either of them has ever waxed. There are dark patches of pubic hair between their fleshy thighs. Marie has a slight paunch to her stomach, a few long, angling stretch marks. Her friend has a similar round body. I imagine they were pregnant at the same time, only Marie's friend looks like she's had more than one child. When she lies back she makes a grunting sound as if all her bones were settling. She has many stretch marks; there is a sunburst tattoo around her navel.

Emily developed terrible striae when she was pregnant. She tried every lotion and balm, but nothing helped. *It's caused by the tearing of the dermis*, she told me, running a hand over her bulbous stomach. Her breasts were so large and tender, it hurt to wear a bra at all. Her ankles and calves swelled.

An attendant squeezes a gooey substance into my hand, speaking in Italian.

Hannah whispers, "Black olive soap. Rub it on your body, but not on your face."

The soap is oily, with a dense, earthy perfume. I watch Hannah spread it along her slim limbs, over her flat stomach and pert backside. Such confidence. Emily was the same way. Unfazed by being looked at, whereas I was more inhibited. One of us had to be. Hannah even has the same narrow hips and slight bowleggedness. She shaves the pubic area, which looks bumpy and chapped, like just-plucked chicken skin.

I stay seated on my towel and work the soap down my neck, feel the mole at the base, the delicate skin in the front. My collarbone feels more protruding than usual, and my breasts, loose. How embarrassing. Had I really shown them to Donato? I try to remember how it felt when I was young and naked in front of Guy. But usually it would happen without me having to get undressed. He could slip my underwear off easier if I was in a dress or skirt, which was how he liked me. Those first two years of our relationship there was a sense of the clandestine, as if my nakedness were tinged with danger. *We cannot get caught*, he would breathe. *Hurry, hurry, let me help you.* He continued to prefer me that way, even after we told my parents about us. I remember how puzzled I was by my mom's reaction. Dad frowned a little and said nothing. But Mom, she looked surprised, in the way that someone is surprised by their own strength. It made her feel good, I think, to have a young daughter who could romance a man whose career was just taking off. It was the only time I felt disgusted by the whole thing.

I look at Marie, who is standing now, and lathering her body with the soap—that belly, which had once carried Donato. Her extra weight is sensuous. There is no denying it. Other women steal glances in her direction. She's short, with petite hands and feet. Maybe she was a runner at some point, she has beautiful calves, a plump round ass. Her breasts are larger than mine, the areolas dark. How easy it is for her to be naked. Casual in her manner, luxurious in her lathering and rubbing of herself. It is erotic watching her. *Vo-lup-tu-ous.*

After a few minutes we dip gold bowls in the running water, pouring them over one another. No one talks, we do not even make eye contact, except fleetingly. The attendant collects us one at a time. I go first, following her to another side room. She tells me to lie down and, using the gloves I bought, scrubs my arms and legs until my skin is electric and tingling. At my stomach she hesitates and then is so gentle she might as well be tickling me. What does she see there? That I've never had children? She's just as careful around my breasts, and I wonder how they compare with others she's seen. What did Donato think when he saw me? I replay that dark expression, uncertain now. I feel my face flush, but the lighting is so dim I don't think she can tell. "Turn over," she says. I'm obedient, and she quickly scrubs my backside. When she's done she tells me in stilted English to shower.

After, I'm led into a third room with a large pool. The attendant hangs a robe on one of the hooks, motioning that it's for me. When she leaves, I'm alone except for the sound of water, which cascades from a lion's mouth. I have not swum naked since Emily was alive. When she was pregnant she wanted to swim in the Pacific during the full moon. How could I say no? She was so uncomfortable, swimming was the only thing that gave her any relief. At the water's edge she coaxed me into undressing. *Don't worry, Cilla*, she said. *We're the only ones here.* We walked into the surf, Emily hesitant and awkward because of how large she was. *Give me your hand*, I said. She followed me out for once. How free it felt, cresting a wave in the nude, the moon lighting up the water and our bodies like diamonds.

I hear splashing. Marie's friend smiles timidly. "Ciao," I say. "This is very relaxing." She nods.

"Your son went to school with Donato?" I try again.

"Donato, *sì*," she says. "*Un bel ragazzo*."

She motions to my stomach, speaking in Italian. I imagine she is asking if I have children. I shake my head. "*Zia*," I tell her.

She gives me that look, the one that says there is a divide between women who have children and those who do not. She is privy to something I can't understand. But I was there for Emily's labor. I know what that part of it was like. They gave her Pitocin almost the moment they got the IV in. Hours went by, the nurses coming in and out to check her dilation. Paul trying to keep her breathing even. Then they put a balloon in her cervix. She was in a tremendous amount of pain. She kept looking at me as if I might be able to do something. I took her hand, talked nonsense into her ear. About the baby, about the new menu at the restaurant we liked on the pier. Anything, because they could not get her epidural in and she was crying and digging her nails into my hand. The drugs helped, but only for an hour or two.

Marie is in the pool now. She speaks to her friend in Italian.

"How was your treatment, Cilla?" she asks me.

"Wonderful," I say, and pretend to be so relaxed I have to keep my eyes closed.

After the epidural everything happened quickly. There was blood, a lot of blood. Paul turned white. The doctor ran into the room, shouting orders to the nurse, and then Emily was carted away for an emergency C-section.

"Oh, that was heavenly!" My niece splashes into the water.

I keep my eyes shut. I don't want to remember how after the birth Emily would not hold the baby. She could not change her diapers. Then Hannah developed thrush and gave it to Emily. They had to be kept separate while the medicine did its work. Emily tried pumping, but the milk was sparse, an hour of pumping produced only an ounce of milk. Her nipples started to bleed. She eventually abandoned breastfeeding altogether.

I remember sitting in their master bedroom, watching Emily change her soiled nightgown. *I still leak*, she said with disgust. I didn't know if she meant from her breasts, or the incision, or from her vagina.

She was examining herself in the full-length mirror. Her belly looked like loose-hanging dough, a grotesque gash stitched across her lower abdomen. She was wearing mesh hospital underwear. I could see the oversize pad, the tiny spider veins along her upper thighs. Her breasts were tightly wrapped in an effort to dry up the remaining milk. *Ruined*, she said, examining herself. *She has taken everything from me.* I thought she might cry, but instead she laughed.

"Do you think my skin will look like that when I'm old?"

I open my eyes and Hannah is sitting next to me in the water, examining her arm against mine.

I must give her such a look, because she says, "Jeez, I was just wondering." I swim to the steps and get out, saying something about being dizzy. But I did not want her to keep looking at the sunspots, the freckles, the thin crepey skin. I don't want to see Marie and her friend's nakedness anymore. I don't want to be reminded of the differences between us.

———

Club Fluid is subterranean, beneath the Villa Borghese Gardens. I can hear the bass thumping from the parking lot. Marie and her girlfriend are in line beside me, speaking in Italian excitedly.

Isn't it awkward to go to a club with your son? I had asked Marie, who had showered quickly when we got back from the spa and returned to Paul and Hannah's in a breezy wrap dress. I was struck again by her overwhelming femaleness. Her full breasts and petite waist. Her skin was glowing.

Romans love to have a good time at any age, she'd said, twin chandelier earrings almost brushing the tops of her shoulders.

"I'm so excited," Hannah says, grabbing my hand. Her two British girlfriends are here too, towering over us in their stilettos.

"Papa never lets me go out this late." She kisses me on the cheek. "It's only because you're here."

It's a mild evening, but the air is electric. It's as if every young Roman was cooped up during the hot afternoon, and now the boys have slipped into their starched dress shirts and tight designer jeans—the girls in anything that will flatter their long, slim limbs and robust cleavage. Nearly everyone is smoking.

I almost didn't come. During dinner I was tired. I had trouble keeping up with the conversation. When Marie's friend got a phone call, I watched her face brighten and I thought, with interest, maybe it was a lover.

Her son, Marie said, leaning toward me. *He's already at Club Fluid with Donato.*

I imagined seeing Donato there, with Marie nearby. I made an excuse—I was exhausted from the spa, from the morning spent at the catacombs. But Hannah pleaded with me. *Please, please, Cilla. Please.*

And then Donato texted as I was getting out of the shower.

—*Coming tonight?* it read.

—*Who is this?* But already I suspected. That warmth stirring.

—*Donato.*

I grasped my towel tighter, looked across the courtyard at his window. But it was dark.

—*There are VIP tickets at the front for you all.*

Heat in my chest as I wondered how to respond.

—*See you soon*, Hannah replied, adding a kissy emoji.

I had been so thrilled to see a foreign number, I hadn't noticed she'd been included too. Nevertheless I could not resist going. I even let Hannah do my makeup.

"There's Donato!" Hannah cries, pointing and trying to get his attention.

I spot him at the front of the line with the bouncers. Silvia is with him, her hair brushed into a pomp; the halter dress she's wearing has cutouts at the waist. Donato's arm is casually draped over her shoulders. His crisp collared shirt is very tight; I can make out every lean muscle.

"Donato, Donato," Hannah calls, waving.

He comes over to us, kisses his mother and her friend on their cheeks. They laugh and smile, slapping him playfully when he flatters them in Italian. I can tell Hannah is waiting for her turn. She blushes when he spins her.

"*Bellissima*." He whistles.

When he looks at me it's with the same calculated charm. Only he's quick about it, he does not mention the silk crepe dress I'm wearing, the one from the shop on Via Condotti. He does offer me a cigarette.

"Cilla doesn't smoke," Hannah reminds him.

He smirks. "Ah, *sì*. I forget. Ready to go in?" He gives us wristbands that will get us free drinks, and then ushers us from the line, past the bouncers and into the club.

It is an instant assault of grinding bodies, of a thick, not unpleasant heat. Flashing lights—blue, white, pink, purple. I can't make anything out. And then Hannah and her girlfriends are gone. Donato too. I look around, but I've been left with Marie and her friend.

"Donato reserved us a booth," Marie shouts to me, and signals that I should follow her.

I push my way through the crowd. Everywhere are women, most not older than thirty, all of them red-lipped and kohl-eyed, with delicate sloping noses, bare shoulders and legs. They are dancing almost on top of one another, their teeth bright white and perfect. A bartender comes by with shots for anyone who will kiss him. Marie's friend leaves a fat lip print on either cheek. *Bacio, bacio*, she mouths to me. I shake my head. *No, thank you*.

A waitress takes us past a velvet rope, to a big round booth where a bottle of champagne sits in a bucket of ice. Marie and her friend are beaming.

Marie leans over to me. "Is this like Los Angeles clubs?"

I nod my head, although I have no idea.

Just then sparklers are lit, and the DJ stops the music. Cristiano is standing on the bar, friends on either side of him. Marie's friend is hollering and whistling and waving frantically.

"The one on the right is her son," Marie tells me. "Donato's best friend."

He isn't as good-looking as Donato; his eyes are smaller and closer together. Even in the poor light I can see acne. I recognize him, though, as one of the boys at Silvia's, when we were drinking on her terrace. I can't remember his name, maybe something biblical.

I want to go to Malibu and eat at Neptune's Net, he had said to me when he learned where I was from. *Like Keanu Reeves in* Point Break.

The boy motions for the crowd to cheer, and they do. It is thunderous. Silvia is in the DJ booth now, I recognize that outrageous pomp. She plays what must be an Italian rendition of "Happy Birthday." Everyone is singing along. Waitresses saber bottles of prosecco, spraying Cristiano. Silver confetti falls from the ceiling. The music launches again, and the sleek young mob dances feverishly, arms in the air.

My head throbs along with the bass. Why had I agreed to this? I plug my ears with my fingers. I feel ridiculous beside these twenty-somethings. Marie and her friend apparently do not. They're drinking the champagne and bopping their heads to the music. I watch a group of girls pucker for a photographer. They're practically falling out of their tops.

I hear Emily's voice. *Prude.*

"I have to go to the bathroom," I tell Marie, and slide out of the booth. And I'm thinking of those catacombs, seemingly endless. I can see Emily, the version of her in that coffin. *Embalming, the displacement of blood and interstitial fluids by embalming chemicals.* I had looked the process up, after Mom insisted on a viewing. *She was so beautiful*, she cried. *I want to see her one more time.* The body is washed in disinfectant, limbs are massaged and manipulated, eyes glued closed, mouth and jaw secured with wires. The embalming solution contains dye to simulate a lifelike skin tone. A warm peach tone, the funeral director told us. I could barely stand it.

I make my way to the second floor, where the music isn't techno, only sultry R&B. There are couches tucked away from the dance floor. I can sense bodies roiling atop them. I look away when I realize I'm staring.

"Cilla." Donato slips his arm around me. "You don't have a drink." He hands me his, which is bright blue and frothy.

"Thank you," I say, and drink the whole thing because I can feel the heat of his hand through the silk of the dress. "Where's my niece?"

"You are not having fun?" he says, grinning.

"It's a long time since I've been to a club. It's louder than I remember."

I catch him glance at my chest and want to crow to all the young half-clothed girls dancing. *I am triumphant.*

"Come dance," he says, taking my hand.

He maneuvers us into the center of the dance floor. I look around to see if Hannah or her girlfriends—or anyone—is watching. "Relax," he says. I laugh when he pretends to be stiff. "Like this," he says, shaking out his limbs. He puts his hands on my waist. *Rilassati*. I breathe in and try to mimic his movements. Beneath the red lights he looks more tempting. "*Rilassati*," he reminds me. *Slowly, slowly.* I close my eyes. Is he wearing cologne? I tilt my head closer. His leg is between mine, he presses up into me and runs his hands down my sides—ribs, waist, hips. He stops there, at my hips, and pulls gently. I catch his eyes, I can see how dark I've made them, how hot and un-even his breathing. Something in me shifts then, and I can feel the weight of his desire, a heavy, serious thing.

I pull away. I want to tell him something about hunger, I want to warn him. But he's smiling, that same playful, teasing smile. So I move my hips, God help me. I close my eyes and tilt my head so I catch his cologne again. *Closer, closer*—there is the scent of my own breath against his skin too. I imagine, I fantasize. In the space between his collarbone and neck, from his jaw to his mouth—I allow myself to pretend. Where's the harm in that? Rome is the original Hollywood.

———

One afternoon Donato isn't at the park, nor is he waiting at the little café. I start and delete at least ten different text messages before deciding not to send him any at all. I had gotten used to the pace of things. The early mornings when I listened to Paul and Hannah get ready, the blow-dryer, the kettle, the dropping of keys. Then the midday heat, when everything is buzzing—the sun, the cicadas, the hustlers and tourists. This is when Donato and I would drink caffè freddos at the park until Han-nah could join us. Soon after that the golden hour—when one Negroni would slip into three, laughter would shift into quick coy glances, and I'd fantasize about letting that heat engulf us both.

When Hannah gets out of class we go for espressos at a café near her school.

"It's only one afternoon," my niece says when I ask if Donato will be meeting us later.

She looks tired. There are dark circles under her eyes. It's her last week of class, and she's in the middle of exams.

"Are you all right?" I ask.

"He's taking Bruce to get shots," Hannah says. Her brows knit together. "Trish says he might go with them to the Aeolian Islands."

My limbs are tingly. I stir another lump of sugar into my espresso. "I thought Donato was coming with his parents and us to Puglia?"

She shrugs. I'm not sure if there is enough blood getting to my limbs. I want to stand up, I need to be moving. The waiter returns with our cornetti. He smiles at us, saying something to Hannah in Italian. I recognize *molto bella*.

"What did he say?" I ask when he's gone.

"That mother and daughter are very beautiful."

We sit and watch the nearby tourists throw coins into a modest fountain, their gelatos dripping onto their wrists. An old man in a tuxedo is playing a cello, the instrument's case open for tips. He pauses to mop his forehead.

"Can I tell you something, Aunt Cilla?" My niece leans forward in her chair.

"You can tell me anything."

She sighs. "I'm in love."

I can taste the espresso, it is threatening to come back up. "Someone I know?"

She giggles. "Donato, of course. Do you think he knows? Do you think he feels the same?"

I can't look at her. I concentrate on breaking apart layers of the cornetto, wiping the cream from my fingers. "It's best not to rush into these things."

She sits back in her chair. "So you don't think he likes me."

But I'm thinking about when Donato showed us the Tarpeian Rock.

This is where traitors were flung to their deaths.

It wasn't a dramatic cliff, only a narrow cobblestone street with cars parked tightly together. I remember mourning doves cooed in a nearby fountain. A pair of butterflies flitted by. But maybe that is betrayal. Sneaky and not how I thought it would look.

"That's not it," I manage. "It's just that he's a lot older than you."

"Hardly," she says. "And what about you and Uncle Guy?"

The look she's giving me. Maybe Emily did tell her the truth about us after all. "It was a different time," I start.

"You know, I don't think Mom liked him. She thought you could do better."

A flash of anger. What did Emily know?

I clear my throat. "Has he . . . have you and Donato been intimate?"

Hannah bursts out laughing. Her whole face is pink and she's biting at her lips. She cannot get ahold of herself. When the waiter comes back with the bill she breaks into giggles again and I have to look away. Clearly, she has not been intimate with *anyone*.

"Oh, Aunt Cilla," she says when she finally gains control. "You saw our first kiss—you were there. You took a picture for us. I felt it down to my toes."

"While I was here," I repeat.

"Well, it sort of started last summer," she says. "When we went to Florence with our parents." She tells me about how Donato took her to his favorite gelato place, and how afterward he bought her the chain at a nearby shop. She pulls out Emily's pendant from beneath her shirt, fingers its gold chain. *Eighteen karat gold*, she reminds me. I feel nauseated.

"Will you ask the waiter to refill my water glass?"

"The funny thing is," my niece continues, not hearing me, "I thought we were just friends!"

Donato does not meet us for drinks later, even though Hannah texts him.

"Maybe try one more time?" I urge. "Let him know I'm buying the first round."

He is not at dinner either, despite both his parents arriving with a bottle of amaro, Paul pouring tiny glassfuls while they talked about grant research and visa paperwork. Why speak in English if I don't know or care what they're talking about? I thought of Hannah and Donato's kiss—how he wrapped her in his arms, Hannah tilting back a little, her eyes closed. I don't want to picture it, but I do. Over and over. Sometimes with music crescendoing.

I feign a headache and go to bed early. Twice I get up and go to the window to see if the light is on in his room. I take four Advil PMs and drift into a dark dreamless sleep. I have a hard time waking up. There is the sound of Hannah's blow-dryer, roaring, and the kettle screeching. The front door slams, my eyes open. I listen to the bolt lock. Hannah's and my brother-in-law's footsteps echoing in the stairwell. Then silence. I roll over, over and over. The pillow lengthwise, below my knees, on my face to block out the sunlight. But I can't get comfortable. Someone is knocking at the door now. Paul and Hannah might have locked themselves out, or maybe it's another apartment altogether. But then I hear him, "Cilla, Cilla, *buongiorno*!"

I hurry downstairs, that heat rekindling. There waiting in the hallway with Bruce is Donato. "Get dressed," he says. "We will have breakfast."

———

"I'm a little upset with you," I tell him after we're seated in the courtyard of the Hotel de Russie. The waiter brings us Americanos and a basket of pastries.

"Me?" He spreads a glob of jam onto a scone. "Ahh, you missed me yesterday." He stuffs it into his mouth.

"You are so full of yourself," I tell him, which makes him laugh that big boyish laugh. I try to ignore the inquisitive stares. It's a certain type of patron here. Plastic surgery, expensive jewelry and watches. It reminds me of the crowds in Hollywood restaurants, where everyone is looking at everyone else. I can feel them thinking it. *Mother and son? She could be old enough. But then again, maybe it is something else* . . . It had been the same with Guy, but not to this extent. It's different when the woman is older.

"It's because . . ." My voice falters. I watch Donato suck a bit of jam off his thumb. I want to ask about Hannah. I want to tell him to stop flirting with my niece. But he looks very young. My phone vibrates, Hannah is calling. I silence it.

The table beside us has stopped talking. The woman looks away when our eyes meet.

"Are you coming to Puglia with us?" I ask.

Donato grins. "Do you want me to come?"

"If you're busy with Silvia, I understand."

He leans forward so that we are very close. I watch a muscle in his forearm twitch as he caresses my hand. "I will be there," he says.

"How is everything?" the waiter asks, and I sit back so abruptly that I bump the table, spilling my Americano.

At the park, Hannah is already waiting for us.

"Where have you been?" she asks. "I called you both."

"I'm sorry." I pull my phone out. "I accidentally silenced it."

I've missed three calls from Guy. I can feel the color drain from my face.

Donato's smile is sly, taunting, when he says to my niece, "Cilla and I were having breakfast."

Guy's phone goes straight to voice mail. What if something happened? I'm breathing quickly, ignoring Hannah and Donato who are talking in Italian. I leave a message for Guy, *Call me when you get this*. Maybe he's e-mailed.

"Are either of you going to ask how my final was?" Hannah is saying.

My e-mail won't load. The signal is weak, and I've forgotten to charge my phone, the battery is about to die.

"Cilla," Hannah cries. But I'm already flagging down a cab.

"I have to get back to the apartment," I tell her. Donato reaches for my arm but I shake him off. "Everything's fine, but I have to go." My voice sounds high-pitched.

I have been neglecting my mom. "Please hurry," I tell the cabdriver. I'm remembering when her physical therapist called a few days ago while we were in the Pantheon—I didn't walk outside to take the call.

She's doing very well, he said.

Could you speak up? A choir was singing an impromptu hymn. Hannah was in awe, her hands folded together. Donato looked back at me—he could be a sculpture himself.

She may be able to come home a little early.

What? I said. *What are you saying? She's supposed to be there for six weeks.*

Ms. Messing, the physical therapist said, clearing his throat. *This isn't a hotel. When your mom is better she has to go home.*

I could see it then, I could feel it. The end of this trip. The oxygen tanks, the wheelchairs, the eventual diapers and twenty-four-hour caregiving. I said something about the connection being bad. *I can't hear you, I'll call back later.* But of course, I never did.

Outside the apartment I struggle with the key. I think I can hear Paul inside, only that can't be right. He's at the university until late, like always. I recognize the voice almost as soon as the door opens, before I even see Guy, who is sitting on the couch, feet on the coffee table, cell phone pressed to his ear.

—

"It's such a mess," Guy says, sitting on the edge of my bed. I've brought him to my room because I'm worried Hannah and Donato are right behind me. And the thought of Donato seeing Guy—their *meeting*—is unbearable. Because I've forgotten some things about Guy. How tight his jeans are, for one—expensive, which I'm sure would impress Donato, but ridiculously tight for a man almost sixty. And that waft of cologne, the oversize Omega watch—the thinning hair, the round, somewhat protruding gut. The way he bites his nails when stressed. I'd forgotten how phony he comes off on first impression. Old and phony.

He's already assured me that Mom is okay. *No, no, nothing like that. She's fine. The nursing home is taking good care of her.* Then

I thought maybe he had come to surprise me. We used to talk about going to Europe together—when I was a lot younger. To Paris or the Amalfi Coast. A twinge of dread, how could I leave now? But he's here because his film is over budget and a potential investor is docked in Porto Turistico on a yacht. *He's a fan of your dad's*, he had pleaded. *Come with me to convince him. I need you.* A strange mixture of relief and disappointment.

"I'm in a real bind," he says, keeping his hands in his lap.

"Well, I have dinner plans."

He fiddles with the A/C unit.

"It's so warm in here. I thought Paul would put you up in a hotel. I mean, you came all this way to babysit his daughter. Do you want me to get you a hotel room?"

It's discombobulating seeing him here. Filling my little room with the scent of him, touching my things, looking at the view from the window. He is supposed to be in Los Angeles, which had felt, until he arrived, far, far away. I glance across the courtyard, to Donato's window, and then pull the curtains closed.

"Hannah's my only niece," I remind him.

"I know," he mumbles. He spots my collection of postcards sitting on the desk. "And quite the little tour guide. Have you really been to all these places?" He holds up a postcard I bought at a museum gift shop at the Capitoline Museums. It's a copy of a Greek statue, a nude boy. I had liked the symmetry, the harmony of the angles.

"Is this one for me?" he asks, grinning. Such a familiar grin. It should shift something in me but doesn't.

"Yours is in the mail." I take the stack from him.

He gets up, examining the rest of the room. He has the kind of swagger that men have when they know they look good on paper. "Is this Hannah?" He's picked up a framed photo of her.

"Goddamn, she's a looker. Do you think she has any interest in film? I could get her—"

"I don't think Paul would like that," I say, taking the photo from him.

He changes tactics then, putting his arms around me. "You look fantastic, by the way. Italy agrees with you."

I can smell the Tic Tacs, the Romeo y Julieta cigars—and that cologne, which feels abrasive now. "It'll be like old times. You and me—closing deals."

"Fine," I tell him. Because I need to get him out of here fast.

He waits while I shower and pretends to sneak a peek when I dress.

"What?" he says. "Can you blame me? You look damn good in this light."

Downstairs a town car is waiting for us.

"You knew I'd say yes?" I ask him.

He slips his sunglasses on, smiling at me. "You're my go-to gal."

We head out of the city, toward the port. Guy pointing out ruins—the Colosseum, a basilica, the Aurelian Walls.

"Remember when you said you'd take me to Italy?" I ask.

He takes my hand and kisses the palm. "We were so young. But hey—we finally made it."

I *was so young*, I think. Outside my window, graffiti-covered storefronts and cafés and apartment blocks whiz by. He's kept hold of my hand, which has begun to sweat.

"All your mom wants to do is talk about the past," Guy is saying. "Every time I saw her these last few weeks it was 'Do you remember when . . .'"

He's rolled his window down, puffing on a cigarillo.

The smell reminded me of when he let me try one. Actually, he offered it to Emily first, and I remember being so jealous that I lied and said I smoked them all the time. *Give me my own.* He must have known I was lying, I couldn't have been older than twelve. Which would have made Emily nine. I slide my hand out from his grip.

"Sorry, was I making you hot?" he says.

Another thing I remember, how upset Emily was when I told her about us. *But he's practically our uncle!* Jealous, I had thought, and I told her so. This male presence in our lives, who had been the focus of our youthful flirtations, was in love with me. That's how I had told her. *Guy and I are in love.* I had wanted someone to confide in and was hurt that my sister did not want to hear any of it. *Gross!* she cried, when I told her that yes, we were having sex. *Are you careful?* she asked, and I thought she meant did we use condoms. *Of course we use protection*—but the look she gave me made me blush. *Don't tell Mom and Dad,* I said. And to her credit, she never did. But something changed between us. She steered clear of Guy at parties, and by proxy, steered clear of me too.

"I really appreciate this," Guy says, grinning that familiar grin. "I owe you."

Seeing him like this, swooping in not because he's worried about me, but because he needs me to vouch for him again—it leaves a bitter taste in my mouth. I pretend not to see his outstretched hand when we've reached the port and he tries to help me from the car.

I follow him down a boardwalk cluttered with families and retired couples in bathing suits, their skin shining and pink. I can make out a meager swatch of beach that looks hard and dirty. The air is humid and reeks of a baking-hot harbor. All seaweed and salt.

"Ciao, Ms. Messing," the investor says when I step onto the boat, which is wide and expensive and exactly the kind of boat you want an investor to own. "This is a real honor."

Hollywood is an easy sell, that's what Guy doesn't get. No outsider ever does. *Everyone wants to believe*, our dad used to say. *A producer might feign reservation, but all it takes is the right kind of confidence.* And Dad was excellent at pretending. It's why there were always parties at the house. *Let the good times roll*, Mom used to say.

I remember once being invited to an opening of a photography exhibition. A friend of our parents', who had been unknown, had become someone important. As so often was the case. Another of Mom's proverbs: *Better to be kingmaker than king.*

Emily and I went to the show with Guy. We must have been seventeen and twenty years old. The two of us arrived in Chanel dresses borrowed from our mom—cameras flashing, everyone eager to meet us.

"Your parents' parties are legendary," Guy's investor is saying to me. He pours me more prosecco.

"Oh, the stories I could tell you," I play along.

It's a different kind of inheritance. A sort of calling card. *You are the daughters of Elliot and Louise Messing.* And poof, just like that, we were in. Emily's brief modeling career was because of it, my stint as a producer too. It's why I know how badly an outsider like Guy's investor wants in, and why I can make the price feel like a steal.

"Dad taught Guy everything he knows," I tell him. "My mother doted on him. He's part of the family."

It's easy to play the part when everything feels like a production. The discerning investor and his pruned Pomeranian, the grilled razor clams with lemon halves wrapped in cheese-cloth, twine tied around the ends in little bows. And the prosecco in delicate crystal glasses, never mind that we're on a yacht and if one were to break it would make a terrible mess—Hollywood is about the aesthetics.

But you can only pretend so much. That photography exhibit—Emily and I passed around the room, chatting and chatting until I thought I could not hear my own voice another minute. Photos of us on the walls—as children, playing naked in the sand; in the arms of a young starlet; examining a toy in a smoke-filled room. Or later, no longer little girls but not yet women, how the angles changed and became more objectifying. I remember one titled *Mother and Daughter* and there was Emily, hair done up like Mom's. They were in matching bikinis, identical smiles and flashing blue eyes. Even their toes in the sand looked identical. The car ride home that night was roaring silence. How exhausted I felt, how empty. I remember hearing Emily in the backseat quietly crying.

I tell the investor stories meant to make him feel part of the fold.

"You can never tell anyone I said this but . . ."

He is enraptured, I can tell by the way he laughs and leans forward, how he makes sure my glass is filled. We are playacting, I want to tell him. *You poor fool.* Guy's hand on my knee, his thumb stroking. None of this is real. I miss Rome, I miss Donato. His eyes on me.

"This movie is going to win every award," I tell the investor, because if I learned anything from those long-ago parties, it's that everyone is looking for the one thing that will have made their living worthwhile.

"It will be your legacy," I say, tipping the last of the prosecco into my mouth.

On the way back into the city, Guy is the quiet one. I roll down my window, so I can cool my flushed cheeks. The sun is setting and the whole lush countryside is blushing pink and purple.

Guy puffs on a cigarillo. "Thank you, Cilla," he says, blowing the smoke out like a big sigh. "You were wonderful."

I can feel the energy slipping from me. I've forgotten how depleting a performance like that is. The depression that sets in afterward. It's reminded me of every boardroom meeting or studio visit or Hollywood party where I had to work the room. How afterward my hands would shake, and sometimes I'd cry on the drive home. That kind of loneliness is sharp.

"It was easier when I was younger," I say, rubbing my temples.

He smiles at me a little, his eyes welling up. "You were always my good luck charm. Christ, look at me. I'm a mess."

Something in me relents a little. I remember how gawky-looking he was when we were younger. Scruffy beard and big ears, how he thought mock turtlenecks were fashionable. We have a history, an understanding, which is more than most relationships.

"Come here," I tell him, and he does, which is awkward because he's bigger than me and we're still in the backseat of the town car. But I manage to wrap my arms around him and press my face into his hair, kissing the top of his head. "And you were always the emotional one."

He laughs, twisting to look at me. "I'm getting worse in my old age."

I must know every line in his face. The crinkles at the corners of his eyes, the lines around his mouth, even the ones etched into his forehead and neck. I used to think of him, but now, alone at night, it's Donato's boyish face I see. Those plump round lips touching my throat, my breasts. I'll close my eyes, and there he is, hovering above me. But it's a losing race. I'll be panting and fantasizing, his mouth here, there—I'll be on the verge, but then anxiety overcomes. The creeping suspicion that I may no longer be a sexual creature.

"Now you look like the one about to cry," Guy says, touching my cheek.

"I'm tired too," I say.

—

It's dark by the time we reach Rome. We pass the Colosseum again, now lit in gold and white lights. The streets are damp and shining from a sudden rain shower. It's humid, the air thick and smelling of exhaust.

We eat at the St. Regis, in the mirrored ballroom beneath glowing chandeliers. There are potted ferns everywhere. Frescoes on the arched ceilings, the color so rich they look cartoonlike and cheap. Everything is gilded. When we're seated I realize the chairs are actually plastic, not lacquered wood—and those mirrored walls have been treated, made to look aged. There is a phoniness to the room, a feeling of something that was once grand, now poorly modernized.

Guy orders champagne, but then looking at me he changes his mind. "Bring us two large whiskeys before you bring us anything else."

The drink does me good. At first, I think it isn't working, the headache is worse than before, the room more vulgar and repulsive, but then suddenly I'm drunk. The gaudy pomp starts to grow on me, I feel affection toward the other patrons—the well-dressed Arabs, the women in their beautiful silk hijabs and chunky jewels, the older couples, even the white-haired woman across the room who is staring and smiling because she thinks Guy and I are younger versions of she and her husband.

I take Guy's hand after the appetizer of sea bass ceviche, after Guy asks if I want another whiskey.

"Or would you prefer to see the wine list?"

"Wine list," I say, smiling, and he smiles too.

We drink a bottle of Gewürztraminer from Alto Adige, and then with the main course a bottle of Chianti from Tuscany.

"I see why you look the way you do," he says, motioning to me with his glass.

I sit straighter, run my fingers through my hair. "What do you mean?"

"You are in love with Rome," he says. "And it is in love with you."

The chef sends out a special for us—a tiramisu with ginger jelly and chocolate flakes.

"Oh, yummy," he says.

And I can tell by his eyes, by their watery sheen, that he will try to take me up to his room.

I take a large sip of wine. "How is Trudy?"

He offers me the last of the tiramisu, and when I shake my head he scoops it into his mouth and relaxes into his chair, patting his stomach. "Let's not talk about her," he says. "I'm here with you."

He's taken my hand, moved it to below the table, onto his leg.

"A nightcap first?" I ask, and he calls the waiter over and orders us two cognacs.

I don't want to think of the effort it will take. The layers of clothes to take off; the hope that I can make him hard, that I will get wet. Sex with Guy sounds exhausting. But haven't I wanted this? For years now, I've been waiting for him to turn back to me.

He swipes the check from the table. "I owe you enough," he says, slipping the waiter his card.

In the elevator he kisses me, almost hungrily. "Cilla, Cilla, you're still so beautiful. Do you know that? So beautiful," he says against me.

I try not to think of anything. *I have wanted this for so long*, I remind myself again. I catch sight of us in the glossy elevator doors. Guy buried in the shallow of my neck, my eyes nearly closed. Do we look like that old version of us? Could I be seventeen again? I slip my hands into his pants, something I would not have done a decade ago—not in a public space. His eyes widen and he lets out a pleased groan.

It goes exactly how I feared it would. After thrusting and grunting, after we have both worked up a sweat and I've tasted the Chianti and the ginger from the tiramisu, he goes limp in me. Then, when he's worked himself back up, I am dry. He spits onto his fingers, working it around. I try not to look disgusted, try not to say right then, *Enough*. I pant and sigh and bounce around until he comes with a tender shudder and a grating of his teeth.

"Did you come?" he asks, rolling over.

Hmm-hmm.

"You really are beautiful; you do know that, don't you?" he says, still out of breath. He sits up, making the sheet slide off him. I can see his flaccid penis, limp in the condom, resting against his thigh.

"I got the good sister," he says, kissing my arm. He gets up and crosses the room bare-assed to the bathroom.

"What do you mean by that? The *good* sister."

"You know," he calls. I hear the shower turn on.

I wince a little when I stand. I'll be sore tomorrow. "No, I don't."

He's sitting on the toilet. "Hey," he says, covering himself with a towel. "Some privacy would be nice."

"I've seen it before. Tell me what you mean by the good sister."

Under the fluorescent lighting he looks older and heavier.

"You know how Emily was—she could have been a genuine child star. I set up an audition for her once, it would have made her. But nothing I did was good enough." His face takes on a bitter slant.

"When was this?" I manage. "I don't remember that."

He shrugs, his shoulders looking fragile and delicate.

"I don't know, she was probably ten or twelve years old. What does it matter? Instead she grew up to become queen of San Clemente. What a waste." He makes a face and flushes the toilet.

We're both back in bed, Guy holding me. Even after rinsing off, his scent is almost suffocating. The little hairs he trims on his chest prickling against my skin. I don't know why I missed this part most.

"Is that Trudy?" I ask when his phone lights up.

"Huh?" He stirs and lets go of me, reaching for his phone.

"Guy," I say with emphasis. "Is that Trudy?"

For a moment I'm not sure I've said anything. He continues texting. I feel my face get hot. I keep thinking of him saying, *the good sister*. Am I the good sister because I never demanded anything from him? Because I was available?

"Being with Hannah these last few weeks has got me thinking."

"About?" he asks.

"You and me." I can't stand the smile on his face, that he's still looking at his phone. "I was her age when we first got together."

"Were you really? That can't be right."

"It was after my birthday party, when you said I looked like a young Jane Fonda."

He brings my hand up to his face and kisses the back of it. "Who can remember that long ago?"

The phone chimes each time Trudy messages him back. I get up to open the balcony door. The hotel room is climate controlled, and the burst of hot wet air is breathtaking.

"What are you doing? It's miserable out there. Come to bed. My flight isn't leaving until later in the morning."

I think I can make out the Duomo near Paul and Hannah's apartment. I wonder if Donato is awake. What he thought when he heard from Hannah that Guy was in town. If he cared at all. I'm sure Paul told her. Guy had gone to the university first to get a house key. *I want to surprise Cilla*, he told my brother-in-law. Another fool.

"I just remembered." I turn back to the room. "We're taking the early train for Bari in the morning and I haven't packed."

He doesn't object, he even offers to dress and walk down with me. "It's fine, don't get up on my account."

I don't wait for him to say goodbye. I'm in the elevator and then outside, hailing a cab. The bellboys and doorman wishing me *buonanotte* despite it being past two a.m.

At Paul and Hannah's I can't sleep. I shower and pack, but when I lie down all I can think about is Hannah's first birthday party. It was at our parents' house. And I remember standing at the kitchen window with Emily, washing our lunch plates, watching our parents walk with Hannah along the beach.

She's so bright, Emily was saying. *I love watching her discover things.*

I'm glad things are getting easier. I was doing the washing, she the drying. Every once in a while, she'd pause, and I'd have to remind her where a dish went.

From the narrow twin bed, I can see the light changing, hear the cicadas renew their drone.

And then Emily said, *Don't take this the wrong way, but I don't want Guy to be alone with her.*

How enraged I was. We argued but she remained resolute. A panicked awareness sharpened somewhere within me. *He's my boyfriend,* I shouted. *Then you won't see either of us.*

———

The train car is packed with preteens heading to Puglia for some kind of overnight camp. Their energy is chaotic, and the train hasn't yet left the station. Backpacks clutter the aisles, boys are hanging out of their chairs, teasing the girls, who are huddled together. The racket is intolerable, the smell too. I try to catch the eye of the adults sitting with them, but they're busy talking among themselves.

"Cilla, I think our seats are over here," Paul calls to me.

We've reserved a table for four and a pair nearby. One of the girls lets out a hyena-like laugh when I pass by. An Italian boy is tormenting her and her friends.

"The train is packed," I say to Paul, who grunts as he tries to fit his luggage into the overhead bin.

"Here, let me," Donato says to Hannah, and takes her bag. "*Grazie,*" my niece replies prettily.

In the morning, when Hannah and Paul came downstairs they were surprised to see me.

I thought for sure you'd be with Uncle Guy, Hannah said. I didn't give anything away, I pretended it had been a glamorous evening. I exaggerated the yacht, the rich investor.

The most delicious grilled razor clams, I said. *And Italian shell-fish risotto.*

I tried to catch Donato's eye, but he was preoccupied with his phone. He arrived early with his parents, looking younger and more beautiful. *Risotto ai frutti di mare*, he corrected me without looking up.

"Maybe we can upgrade to first class," I say to Paul, who is wiping his hair from his forehead. The train has not yet turned on the air.

"You can certainly try," he says. "But it's probably fully booked. Every Italian is escaping for the seaside."

"Cilla," my niece says, bouncing into the window seat at the table, "you can sit with me."

Tonio and Marie take the seats facing her.

"I brought a deck of cards." She places the pack on the table. "Mom said the two of you used to play."

Fleeting glimpses of when Mom and Dad's partying kept us awake—Go Fish and gin rummy and crazy eights. But I don't want to think of that.

Paul and Donato have taken the pair of seats a few rows away.

"I'm a little hungry," I tell my niece. I steal a glance at Donato, who is texting someone, smiling a coy, secret smile. This depresses me more than the memory of Guy last night in the hotel room. I had paused in the doorway as I left, turned to look at him one last time. The plush wall panels and sconces, the four-poster bed, it could have been the setting of a Renaissance painting. And in the middle of it was an overweight fifty-nine-year-old, hair askew, clutching the sheet over his naked body in case somebody was in the hall.

"I think I'll go see what they have in the café car."

I push past the children who are running around unchecked. I tap a boy on the shoulder to ask him to move. He doesn't understand, and I have to squeeze by him.

The attendant in the café car is young, probably not much older than Donato. I order a vodka and soda. "It is early," he says, pointing to a clock on the wall. I hold his gaze. He produces two miniature bottles and a cup of ice. *"Mille grazie."* I sit at one of the tables and try to compose myself. There's room to breathe here, the A/C is already on, and I have the car to myself. The windows are large, larger than the ones in economy class. I can watch the bustling train station, the rush of passengers hurrying, hurrying. I drink the vodka fast, hoping it will ease the various pains in my joints, the soreness in my groin.

When Donato enters he stops at the bar and then comes over with two newspapers, one in Italian and another in English.

"You left us at the park," he says, sitting across from me. He puts the papers between us, examining their headlines. I'm pretty sure he's pretending to read, because a moment later he looks at me and asks, "Did you have fun with Uncle Guy?"

I struggle to keep from crying out with glee. He's jealous. I clear my throat, lean across the space between us.

"I'm sorry I left you in the park. Guy is just an old friend and he needed my help."

He presses his lips, thinking it over.

I add, "I would have rather stayed with you."

Allora. He grins and goes to buy a split of prosecco at the bar.

"A drink before a journey is good luck." He taps his cup to mine. When he tilts his head closer to me a curl falls forward.

"Let's stay here, there are many children in our car." His gaze falls across my chest. I'm wearing a silk blouse, a camisole underneath, but still I feel him looking at my breasts. "And the views are better."

I can't help it, I smile. "You're impossible." The train lurches, beginning to move.

"Give me your feet," he commands.

"What? No." I laugh nervously—ignoring that he's reaching beneath the table for my legs. I feel his hands groping.

"Donato," I say, but I can hear how breathy I sound. I think of the clichés—of older women and younger men. He is only seventeen. I should pull away, I know. But I don't.

Outside, the city is getting farther and farther behind us. We pass ruins of aqueducts, of cathedrals and basilicas and castles. Farmland spreads out. Wheat fields tall and blond. The train gliding along the track. When I shut my eyes the sunlight speckles the backs of the lids, I can feel heat coming from the window.

His hand has slipped past my ankle, he's stroking the narrow part of my calf. Different from Guy, who would have plunged forward, confident. I can tell Donato isn't sure if I will stop him or not. I'm not sure either. I only know that I like the feeling of his fingers exploring.

A group of Italian boys enter the café car, hollering and roughhousing. Donato drops my leg and I sit up in my seat. The largest of the group is looking over. He has a hawkish nose and beady eyes. An ugly boy. He nods in my direction.

They sit in a booth near us. Two of them have braces. When they smile, I can see the metal contraptions. They look painful, as if they'd cut their delicate inner cheeks. They laugh and yell over one another in Italian. Louder than they need to be.

But then the hulking one with the tiny eyes tilts his head,

brings his shoulders up to his ears, smiles an unsure half smile. Maybe not that unattractive after all. What is *wrong* with me?

I catch the attendant glance over, and I have to look away this time.

"Hannah is probably wondering where I am," I say, standing.

I feel the effects of the alcohol as I make my way through the cars. I'm queasy, but less aware of my sore, aching body. When the train jerks, I brace myself. *Scusami.*

In our car the yelling children, the odor of their prepubescent bodies is heady, like the animal markings left by feral cats.

"Have they still not turned on the air-conditioning yet?" I ask.

Paul has taken the seat beside Hannah. They're playing a card game with Marie and Tonio.

"Cilla," my niece says when she sees me. "Did you find something to eat?"

"Sorry to take your seat," Paul says. He lays a card down on the table.

"We've started a game of bridge," Marie tells me without looking up from her hand.

Hannah rolls her eyes. "Papa is determined to teach me even though it's a game for old people."

Marie clicks her tongue, and the four of them laugh.

The train rushes through a tunnel. The children hoot and holler. I try to unclog my ears but the tunnel stretches on and on. Another train speeds by in the opposite direction. I feel the vibration of the tracks as if it were ricocheting in my bones. *Doe-nat-oh-Doe-nat-oh*, the train beats along.

"The noise," Tonio complains.

At last we emerge. The cabin feels overly bright.

I rub my eyes. "I didn't sleep well last night, I'll try to take a nap."

"Good luck," Paul says, motioning to the group of girls and boys, who are as rambunctious as ever.

The other pair of seats isn't far from them. I can hear Paul and Tonio speaking in Italian. Instructing, I'm sure, Hannah or Marie on how to play the game.

When Donato comes back into the car, I pretend to be asleep. I hear him with the others. He's brought them all snacks. "*Mio figlio*," Marie exclaims. I imagine how she must take him by the face, kissing his cheeks. There is the sound of lips smacking against skin. A rattling of Italian endearments, which I don't understand, but the tone is unmistakable. A proud mother of a beautiful son. He has even brought Hannah's favorite candy bar. "You remembered," she gushes. He stands with them for a while, the five of them speaking Italian—probably discussing the game. Their voices are low and focused. The children have quieted too, the length of the trip having outpaced them.

Outside, the Italian countryside is a blur of farms and vineyards. In the distance smoke billows, streaking the sky red.

"The farmers," Donato is saying. He's leaned across me, so he can see what I'm looking at. "They slash and burn. It is an old practice. May I sit?"

He angles past me and makes himself comfortable in the window seat beside me.

"Or it is Mafia. The Triangle of Death is over those mountains."

"Donato," I start because he's looking at me the same way he had in the café car. "Your parents are right there. Hannah and Paul—"

He grins. "We sleep, all we do is sleep." He drops his head onto my shoulder.

"Donato." I push him away. I try to be stern. "No touching."

He purses his lips. "*Allora*," he says, shrugging. Still there is that teasing smile. He takes off his overshirt, rolling it into a makeshift pillow and sticking it between him and the window.

I strain to look behind us. I can't see Hannah or Tonio, who have the window seats, but I can see Marie, she's concentrating on her hand. And Paul, who's across from her, has his back to me, but I recognize his coat hanging over the chair. Every so often I catch a glimpse of his arm as he plays a card.

At the end of the train car the group of girls who were laughing with the boys are now in deep conversation with one another. Such serious excitement for whatever trip they are on, which will become, like most parts of their childhood, unimportant or forgotten. Unless something happens that defines the moment, this too won't matter.

Donato has his eyes closed. His top lashes are long and dark. The T-shirt he is wearing is very thin; I can see his chest rise and fall with each breath. The pace quickens when I lower the seat tray in front of him, spreading my cardigan over both of us. *It is broad daylight*, I warn myself. But I can't stop now. Under the tray my hand is undoing his belt, which is an easier and quicker task than I thought it would be. There is no time to think. I like the way his face looks while I do the searching. The tiny facial tics, how his tongue wets his lips a little. He slouches farther into the seat so that I can get a better grip. The heat I find there is enough to match my own.

But then I hear Hannah or Marie, or maybe both of them— and I take my hand out of his pants.

I don't know what I'm doing. I get up, I need somewhere quiet. Somewhere away from everyone. There is not enough air in here. That's what it is. The lack of oxygen is to blame. The next car isn't any better. It's just as packed and stuffy. My legs feel weak. My hands have a tremor. Maybe my body is changing after all.

Donato has followed me into the bathroom. He closes and bolts the door. He looks upset. I don't understand a word he's saying. He's only speaking in Italian.

"I'm sorry," I say, pulling him to me. *I'm sorry.* Although I don't know who I'm apologizing to. Marie? Hannah?

Doesn't matter, I'm already kissing him. It could be chaste, forgivable, except for my hands, which are holding his face, grasping at him. How hot my breath is, and I am moving against him. His hands are under my blouse. This should be embarrassing, my tongue is in his mouth. We are in a public bathroom with the toilet water sloshing about from the speed of the train.

"You did this to me," he says, and places my hand on the hard bulge in his pants. I can hear my own breathing, still taste his mouth. We must be going through another tunnel, because I'm light-headed.

All right, I think. *All right.* I undo his belt again, and kneel on the floor. It's easy then. His labored breath, the simple reflex of the motion. Up down, up down. Stroking with my hand, switching to my mouth. He tastes like sucking on the end of a balloon, and then, like sweet salty earth.

"Look at my son." Marie points across the pool, where Donato has climbed an olive tree. His swim trunks cling to his thighs, his hair dripping from his last jump into the water. Behind him the countryside is flat and dotted with more olive trees. When the breeze picks up and their branches bend, I can make out a sliver of the Adriatic, cobalt against the horizon.

"Woohoo!" Donato whoops from the top branch. "I can see Greece from here."

"Jump," Hannah taunts. She's stretched across a pool float looking slim and tan.

"He is showing off," Marie says to me from the table where she's sitting with Paul and Tonio, their papers and laptops surrounding them.

The sun is different here. It has bleached the countryside white: the villages, the roads, the rocks and cliffs along the ocean. *There are only bold colors in Puglia*, Agostina, the *masseria*'s owner, an old friend of Marie and Tonio's, had said when she first picked us up at the Bari train station. And she's right. Against all that white, the ocean is a lovelier teal, the bougainvillea a brighter fuchsia, the palms and olive trees a deeper green.

Splash!

Donato has jumped from the tree into the pool. When he surfaces he shakes his head, sending water everywhere.

"Ahh!" Hannah cries, covering her face.

"*Cucciolo mio!*" Marie exclaims.

He's gotten water on me, too, which had been the point. He swims to the edge of the pool where I'm lying out and hoists himself up. I watch him settle into a recliner, stretching his lean body. Sleek like a seal. Water drips, pooling beneath him. The few hairs on his chest matted and dark. He raises one arm, tucking it behind his head. His sunglasses flash at me.

When we arrived at the *masseria*, several days ago now, we went on a winery tour. The owner was a friend of Agostina's. He showed us his vineyard and we toured the big tankers in the warehouse. Then we hit the wine bar in the *centro storico* of a nearby hillside town, where we could sample the product.

It was easy to slip away from the others when we were all a little drunk and eager to explore. *Many of these towns are circular to confuse invaders*, Donato said as I pulled him along a narrow alleyway. *Paths start and stop.* At any moment we might have run into Paul or Marie or Tonio, or Hannah—who had been the most difficult to shake. *But it never mattered*, Donato was saying. We had found a dim corner, in front of a restaurant that had not yet opened. *They were always slaughtered anyway.* The sun was setting and had turned the limestone and travertine buildings pink. In that kind of lighting he looked radiant.

The next day there was an olive oil tasting at a farm in nearby Fasano, where I could get Donato to myself by falling behind from the others. *There are so many olive trees*, I said when we finally rejoined them. *We got turned around.* Then a cheese-making demonstration in Alberobello—the town's whitewashed stone huts looking like something from a fairy tale. *Trulli*, Donato said, as I pushed him into a café bathroom. *Built by enterprising peasants.* It was easy because what I wanted from him required little time. If only I can hear that quick intake of breath, fill my mouth with his scent.

"Are you coming in, Aunt Cilla?" Hannah calls from the water. "You don't want to lie out too long or you'll end up looking like Papa!"

"Ha, ha, very funny," my brother-in-law says from the shaded patio table. His face bright red, shiny from where he applied aloe. On our last group outing, a bike tour along the coast, Paul got a severe sunburn. It was decided then to abandon the remaining trips Marie had planned. Paul and Tonio are content to work alongside each other now, poolside, while Agostina brings them iced mint tea and plum cake.

"I have sunscreen on," I tell my niece, and roll over so I can better watch Donato without her noticing.

Paul's mishap has left it just the three of us. In the afternoons we borrow the rental car. I insist Hannah take the passenger seat, beside Donato, who does the driving. I make sure she's between us whenever we are together—until she's not. *You guys ditched me, again*, she said, pouting, after the last time we went into the nearby beachfront town.

On the way there, she had been excited, talking about Malibu. *Mom and Cilla used to have beach days when I was little*, she told Donato, who drives with casual abandon, never signaling or honking, simply accelerating around drivers he thinks are going too slowly.

We have a beach house, she said, and that *we* startled me. Hannah and myself. *We* are family. The weight of that—of my responsibility—I suddenly felt it so completely that I looked away when Donato winked at me in the rearview mirror.

After we parked, as we walked to the end of the harbor, which gave way to a curving sandy beach, Donato flirted with Hannah, keeping her gushing at whatever he said or did. I felt duplicitous, and almost feigned a headache so we'd return to the *masseria*. But then down at the water's edge, Donato slipped out of his shirt and dove into the blue-green waves, coaxing us to follow him in. That smile, his boyish good looks. All the women and girls noticed him: the moms with babies playing in the sand; the older women at the beachfront bars; girls on their towels, sunning themselves, hoping he might look back at them. It wasn't just me, they had all fallen under his spell.

It was why I stopped in front of an entirely ordinary shop— blown-up pool floats hung from the ceiling, snorkeling equipment and fins and boogie boards and sand toys cluttered the aisles. *Hannah*, I said. *Let's look in here.*

It was so littered with cheap summer items that I lost her almost instantly. I pulled Donato outside, behind the shop where no one could see us.

There is still a bit of gravel in my shin from kneeling.

"It's too hot," I announce, getting up from my recliner. I can feel Donato watching me. I wish there was more embellishment to my bathing suit. It's a plain black one-piece. I had packed it because at the time I thought it suited a possibly premenopausal aunt. But now I'm embarrassed by how dowdy it is.

Agostina has come out with her grandson, Matteo. He's a quiet toddler with fine blond hair that is so white his tan skin glows beneath it. *Amore, amore.* Marie starts singing an Italian rhyme. Agostina claps along, the baby on her lap. The child is enraptured. He has dimples on either cheek. His eyes are big and an unnerving bright blue.

"I used to sing to Donato when he was a baby," Marie says when she's finished.

"He's very beautiful." I smile at him. *Molto bello.*

"*Grazie*," Agostina says.

I pinch his plump, dimpled cheek. "Ciao, Matteo, ciao." He pushes his face into Agostina's bosom.

"He is shy," she says to me. "Do you want to hold him?"

"Oh, no." I step away. "I was about to go inside."

Marie takes the baby instead and I watch her bounce him on her knee, Agostina smiling and cooing until the baby lets out a bubbly giggle.

"The salt water from the pool has dried funny," Donato says, standing. "I need to shower." He bends to kick water at Hannah as he passes by.

"Hey!" she cries but looks pleased. He grins at her from over his shoulder.

I watch Agostina and Marie play with the baby another moment. On the ground nearby a lizard does a few push-ups, emerald green against the chalky stone. I can smell the sea, saltier than the Pacific.

"This heat makes me so tired." I yawn. "I think I'll lie down until dinner."

Tonio stands up from the table. "I'll walk with you. I need a book that I left in my room."

I feign indifference. *Okay.* I smile.

The pool is a considerable distance from the main buildings. We walk in silence, just the sound of the cicadas and the crunching of our sandals against the loose gravel path. There had been a German couple staying when we first arrived, but they were gone the next day. *We will have the place to ourselves*, Agostina said excitedly to Marie, who clapped her hands.

"It was a monastery," Tonio says finally. "The *masseria*, I mean. Built by Basilian monks in the seventh century."

"Paul mentioned that, it's enchanting." I think I can see Donato, on the other side of the orange orchards, waiting for me at the mouth of a cave where centuries ago those monks pressed olive oil. I recognize the striped shirt. He's left it unbuttoned in the front, wearing it like a jacket, the sleeves rolled up.

"How is your mother?" Tonio asks, holding open the gate that separates the pool area from the car park. "Is she getting well?"

More jewel-toned lizards dart along the dry stone walls.

"She's a fighter," I say. "She'll be fine."

The *masseria* is so remote, phone calls drop. I have not e-mailed either. When I start one the cursor just sits there, blinking. My inbox has piled up with messages—from the landscaper, the real estate broker, the roofer and the exterminator and Guy—I haven't opened any of them.

"I am sure she is looking forward to your return home," he says. I can't see his face, he's looking out toward the sea of olive trees.

"Yes," I tell him. "She is."

My room is the only one in the main house, the others are in what was once the domestic quarters. In the courtyard, where we should part, he pauses to watch me walk the rest of the way.

"See you at dinner," he calls, and waits until I've gone inside.

———

I sit on my bed, listening for Tonio's footsteps walking away. My room is an austere suite, made entirely out of polished stone, with high arches as if it were a basilica in miniature. Agostina wanted me to have her nicest room. *A real Hollywood producer.* She was thrilled. *It must be very exciting.*

What is taking him so long? I peer out the window. There he is, hands clasped behind him, examining an ancient stone well.

The clock in the living room begins to chime, the cicada drone seems louder. I'm watching the sunlight move across the Persian rug. Every moment that goes by is another second lost. Being in Puglia means more than half my trip is over. I don't realize I'm pacing until my phone vibrates.

—*Where are you?*

I check the courtyard for Tonio. There's only wind tangling in the bougainvillea vines, fuchsia and orange blossoms scattering across the ground. I take a split of prosecco from the mini fridge, and quietly, quietly, slip out my door.

—*On my way*, I text back.

To avoid detection, I take the stairs down to the breakfast room and leave from there. It leads to the garden where Agostina grows root vegetables and herbs. My chest is tight, my limbs tingling from committing this subterfuge. I'm reminded of those early days with Guy. Sneaking around, hiding our relationship from my parents. Something to make the blood pump, to make me aware of my heartbeat. A secret all to myself.

The wrought-iron gate separating the garden from the orange orchard is massive and old and creaks loudly when I push it open. I pause to listen for footsteps, but there's only cicadas and honey bees. Some ways off I hear splashing in the pool.

I try not to think of my niece, who has become part of our deception. Emily had played a similar role, albeit a more informed one. *Just say we're going to the movies*, I would beg her. Or that I was sleeping over at the same friend's house as her. *Mom will never know.*

I touch my lip where Donato kissed it yesterday when we were in the parking lot. How his expression changes when he looks at me from across a room. How terrifying and nerve-racking and exhilarating—I pick up my pace, jogging through the orange trees.

"Donato?" The cave is large and dark, with crude rooms cut into it, a round slab in the middle where a donkey would have been attached to a mill.

He sneaks up behind me, wrapping his arms around my waist.

"*Zia* Cilla!"

"Don't call me that," I say, but, really, if it means he'll let me lead him deep into the olive groves, away from the *masseria* and Tonio and Hannah and everyone else—he can call me whatever he wants.

"Was that my *papà* with you?"

"He wanted to tell me the history of the *masseria*." I take his hand. "Did you know it was built by monks?"

"I thought maybe he was on to us." He grins. "Where are we going?"

"On a little walk, or do you not want to?"

He kisses my palm. "*Sì, voglio.*"

The olive trees were planted in vast grids, their trunks large and knotted. The earth around them has been tilled, making the dirt boglike. I can hear him breathing hard behind me. My own heart is pumping fast, I feel it in my temples. My lungs burn.

"Is here good?" he asks, his forehead slick with perspiration. It's that time of day just before the sun begins to set when it feels like there is more sky than earth. The groves are pungent and rich.

"Here in the dirt." I make him sit against one of those ancient tree trunks. He pats the hard ground beside him. "Did you not bring a blanket?" I ask.

"*Mi dispiace.*" He instantly sheds the striped shirt, laying it on the ground for me to sit on.

"I'm teaching you chivalry." I laugh, kneeling on it. "How to be a good man."

We share the split of prosecco, watching the swifts dart over the fields. Then I kiss him. He tastes of sweat and alcohol and something I can't name, but which keeps me up at night.

I've given him my mouth, but his hands want more. They seek entrance to parts of me that I have not given him access to. "Why do you not let me touch you?" he pants. A question I don't have an answer for. Something to do with Hannah maybe, but also Emily and Guy and the fear that I may have limitations as a woman.

Eventually he stops protesting and gives me what I want. Then there is only his labored breath, an occasional Italian word I can't understand and don't want to. His fingers become knotted in my hair so that my eyes water—and afterward, he has to gently, gently untangle them.

I'm following Emily and our mom, down the courtyard path toward the sea. How similar they are from behind, dressed in matching eyelet dresses, their hair swinging at exactly the same pace. How slim and delicate their bodies are, so unlike myself. *You take after your father*, my mom would often lament. One daughter tall, the other petite. It is the same in the animal world. Mockingbirds nested in our orange tree late one spring, and after their two chicks hatched we could hear their harsh *chack*, calling for their mother to feed them. The louder, smaller one always ate first. I can hear the sea crashing—but this isn't the Pacific, it's the Adriatic. There is no mistaking the two, the air here is almost alkaline.

I wake on the rocks near where Hannah, Donato, and I have laid out towels and pads lent to us by Agostina. The hot afternoon must have lulled us to sleep. Donato is curled on one side of me, Hannah asleep on the other. I hear him gently snoring. It is the hour of the *riposo*, when the midday heat is strongest. We are beneath the shadow of a cliff, but even in shade the heat is leaden. A wave crashes against the rocks, the wind catches its spray and sends it toward us.

We spent the entire morning trying to find a beach free of crowds, a near-impossible task. Most places turned us away at the parking lot.

Donato's skin is hot. I lift his hair and blow onto his neck. *Cool down, child*, I think. I can see where the water has dried across his back, leaving smears of salt. I would like to lick him there. Just to know the taste.

He had gotten into an argument at the last beach club we tried. The parking attendant was a boy his own age, shirtless and heavily tattooed. At first Donato was trying to be casual, I could tell by the cadence of his voice. *I am one of you.*

But something about Donato rubs these country boys the wrong way. His expensive collared shirts, his slim build—he is not muscular or tattooed like them. The boy said something in a hardened, biting Italian, so unlike the polished language Donato speaks. Suddenly they were shouting at each other. Hannah joined in, which made the attendant boy guffaw. He pointed at her, and whatever he said made Donato start to get out of the car. I had to insist we leave. He was fuming afterward.

What did he say to you? I asked Hannah as we hiked down to this small cove.

Oh, the usual, she said, looking pleased. *If I want a real man, yadda yadda.*

Lying beside her like this, I can smell her hair. Earthy and rich. Almost exactly the same. It's a strange thing, to know the scent of a sibling. An embarrassing intimacy.

"We should go for a dip," I say, nudging Donato.

He stretches and turns toward me, grinning. "I was having a good dream, you were in it."

"Shhh, don't wake Hannah."

He looks across me, at my niece. That mop of black curls, wild in the light wind.

"You have freckles," he says, tracing my bare shoulder. I like how brown his hand looks against my skin, the soft downy hairs on his forearm.

We have to step carefully: salt deposits have dried, making parts slick. Donato leads the way, hopping from spot to spot. There is one part of the craggy rocks that juts out into the turquoise water. It isn't high, maybe a foot, but I hesitate.

Donato has already dived in; he motions for me to do the same.

The water is very clear, I can see large boulders at the bottom, and the sun reflecting on the surface makes the water seem alive.

"Jump fast," Donato calls. "Or you could get hurt."

I get down on my butt and slide in.

Donato swims over to me. "I thought you grew up on the beach," he says, and kisses me. I look at the rocks where Hannah is still asleep. I can see her bright orange bikini bottom, her T-shirt fluttering in the breeze.

"In Malibu you don't have to jump into the water, you walk right into the surf and swim out."

He's floating on his back, an easy thing to do when the water is so salty and buoyant.

"You can show me when I visit."

I push on his chest so that he sinks. Then he's laughing and swimming after me. That's how Hannah finds us, playing and rolling on top of each other in the sea.

"Hey!" she yells. I shield my eyes from the glare. I think maybe she's frowning, but then she leaps into the water.

Cannonball!

A good way off in the water is a vertical column of white rock. When we first got here, a group of teenagers were swimming near it, a few jumped from the top. *Faraglioni*, Donato had said. *They are made by the sea and wind.* But now the teenagers are gone, and the rock tower looms behind us like a prehistoric ruin.

"Let's swim to it," Hannah says, pointing.

"That's pretty far," I say.

She rolls her eyes at me. "Come on, Donato." She chides him in Italian.

The image of them swimming away: how complementary they are, in both youth and looks, and with that aquamarine sea stretching out around them, the impossibly white *faraglione* rising out of the water—it's searing into my brain.

I swim after them.

At the base of the rock the current is stronger. It smashes me against it with each swell. Hannah has already started to climb, but Donato's waited for me.

"It looked smaller from the shore," I tell him.

"Put your hand here," Donato directs. A swell pushes us together, for a moment our legs intertwine beneath the waves.

"It's too high," I tell him.

"The view is wonderful," my niece shouts from the top.

Another swell, and he uses it to press against me. He's got my earlobe in his mouth. I can feel his tongue, soft and warm.

"Put your foot here," he says, turning me to face the rock. "I will lift you."

With the next swell he lifts me and I'm able to scramble up.

Everything is ocean, the entire horizon. It expands the lungs seeing that much blue. I breathe in, feeling where Donato nibbled on my ear, and the salt water drying like a briny layer of skin that needs to molt.

"Where do you think we should jump?" Hannah asks Donato, once he's joined us.

I can see the goose bumps along her arms and thighs. The wind is stronger up here.

Donato is breathing hard from his climb. He wobbles when he looks over the edge.

"Please be careful." I grab his arm. Then, because Hannah is looking at me, "Your parents would kill me if something happened to either of you."

"Here will be good," Donato says. "Wait for a swell, there might be rocks below."

I can see where our towels are, and on top of the cliff, Paul's rental car. They look tiny and far away. Below, a wave smashes against the rock, spraying us.

"I don't know if I can do it," I say, looking at where Donato is pointing.

But then someone's shoved me and I'm falling. I hit the water hard enough that my ears pop. I stretch my legs out, hoping to shoot off the ocean floor. I kick a rock, hard and jagged, feel it scrape my ankle. I surface with salt water in my eyes, my nose and mouth.

There are two splashes nearby, and when I see Donato's grinning face, eyes glittering, I want to throttle him.

"What were you thinking!" I choke out.

Ha-ha-ha, that childish cackle. "It was Hannah."

"Last one back is a rotten egg!" my niece cries as she swims toward shore.

———

When I come out of my room I hear Marie singing softly. The *masseria*, despite its thick walls, is uncomfortably warm by the end of the day. Usually the group waits in the courtyard for everyone to gather. But there in the living room, the soaring windows thrown open, are Agostina and Marie with Matteo.

"An Italian lullaby," Marie says to me and continues to sing.

The boy is sitting on Agostina's lap, eyes nearly closed, head tilted so Agostina can better comb his hair.

At night, the *masseria* is lit by large ceramic egg-shaped lanterns. Their light along the walls is lacelike from their honeycombed pattern. *Pumo di fiore, a bud about to bloom*, Agostina had explained to me. In Puglia they are a symbol of prosperity, or fertility, or a kind of good luck charm. I could not tell which, the translation got lost somewhere in the middle.

"The combing is good for him," Agostina whispers. I haven't noticed before, but in this light, I can tell she's had work done. Her forehead is unwrinkled, she has swollen, artificial lips. She must be in her sixties. Marie has been staying here since she was a girl. When Agostina first greeted us, she kissed both Marie and Donato right on the lips. *I have known Donato since before he was born*, she had said. *My plum cake is in his blood.*

I can hear the comb, raking over the toddler's head.

"If you can believe it," Marie is saying to me, "Donato was bald at birth. The doctor told me to do the same thing. Now look at him."

"You brush to stimulate the follicles," Agostina says, still combing away. There is a distinct expression of pleasure on her grandson's face, which embarrasses me.

The restaurant is not a far walk, but the fields of olive trees are very dark. We have to take flashlights, and even then, it's hard to see the length of the curving shale road. Without the buildings of Rome, the cicadas are unhindered. They are blaring. Other animals prowl the night too—bats and owls and wild boar. *They sometimes attack children*, Marie had said. She and Agostina keep Matteo between the two of them.

Out in that black our destination looms like a solitary star, lit up by tiny lights strung along the building and vineyard and in the branches of their stately olive trees.

"Was this *masseria* built by monks as well?" I ask Paul, who takes the seat next to mine. Donato is quick about sitting across from me, his father beside him. Poor Hannah is stuck with Marie and Agostina and the baby at the end of the table.

"I'm not sure."

"It looks eighteenth century," Tonio says, surveying the patio, the vine-covered pergola. "A fortified farmhouse, probably."

He asks the waiter in Italian, and then tells me with a grin that he was right. It must be maddening to be married to him. Or to be his son. I see how disparaging he is. Just because Donato's uninterested in books and school, like any young person. *A dreamer*, Marie had defended him. *My little Donatello is a dreamer.* She is constantly treating him like a child, something that I think frustrates Donato more than his father's derisive remarks. *They don't understand me*, Donato complained to me one afternoon. We were in the olive fields, or maybe it was the dark corner of that hilltop ancient town. Time has ceased to matter. I silenced him with my mouth. *Hush*, I murmured. *Let me have you.*

"Ah," Donato says when the waiter fills his wineglass. "This is the life, no?" With a tan he is almost luminous.

When the focaccia comes, still warm, the cherry tomatoes split open from the oven's heat, we tear chunks and eat it, watching one another from behind our wineglasses.

Be careful, Cilla. Be careful. But it's hard to care anymore. It's become difficult to think of anything else other than what's in the foreground: Donato and those twinkling lights in the olive trees just behind him. How easy it is to ignore the darkness in the distance. To pretend that this is all that there is.

Tonio is laughing and wiping at his eyes. "Cilla missed the dance. Cilla, are you watching? Paul, do it again."

"I don't think I can." My brother-in-law is flushed. His forehead is slick with perspiration.

The pastas have come, and I can hear Agostina's fork and knife scrape against her plate as she cuts Matteo's ravioli into bite-size pieces.

"What are you guys talking about down there?" Hannah strains, trying to see us better.

"*Tarantismo*," Tonio says. He's removed his jacket, loosened his tie. But every so often I catch his glasses flashing in my direction. He's paying attention.

"It was a hysteria that took over southern Italy in the sixteenth and seventeenth centuries," Paul tells his daughter. "If you were bitten by a tarantula you had to do a special dance or else you'd die."

Tonio's rolled up his sleeves; his arms are dark and hairy. Such a contrast from his son's. Another thing that must disappoint him. Donato takes after his mother, his body is nearly hairless. "Cancellieri described it as: One cries, vomits, laughs, cries, faints, and suffers great pain before dying—unless you dance."

"Why am I not surprised it's about death." Hannah looks at Donato for commiseration, but he's refilling my wineglass.

"It goes something like this," Paul says, and flails about, arms and hands in the air.

Matteo thinks this is hilarious, and claps his plump baby hands. We all laugh. "Did you like that, Matteo?" Agostina says.

"Wait, I couldn't see." Hannah has stood up from her chair. "Do it again."

Paul lets out a long sigh, wiping his face with his cloth napkin. "I'm too full of wine and risotto."

Matteo holds out some of his food to her.

"Hannah," Marie says, "Matteo wants to share."

Tonio is still laughing. "Your face when you dance."

"Was it originally a Bacchanalian rite?" Paul asks, and Tonio answers him in Italian.

I hear my niece drop into her chair. I imagine her face from dinner in San Clemente years ago, lip tucked into mouth, resigned to being excluded. *I understand*, I want to tell her. She'll have to learn to steel herself from the particular hurt a parent can inflict. I accepted that I wasn't the beautiful daughter. That I would be the one doing the nurturing.

"What is Cilla thinking about?" Donato asks. "I bet I can guess."

I can feel his foot caress the side of mine.

The waiter has brought slices of green melon and ricotta for the table. He's taking espresso and grappa orders. It is very tender, the melon. And cold, as if it were in a fridge right up until this very moment. I can feel it traveling down my throat. The juice gets everywhere, the table, my napkin—some spills onto my lap. The cheese is good as well, firm and just a little salty.

Donato nods his head and then excuses himself from the table. I'm sure that Hannah saw it, because she follows him inside.

"Do you want sugar with your espresso?" Paul asks. He's offering me a sugar packet.

"Yes," I say. "Thank you, I mean, *grazie*."

He smiles, such a reassuring smile. I remember how surprised I was the first time I met him. He was so different from Emily's previous boyfriends. A little boring maybe, but supportive and affectionate—things we had little of growing up.

Something else I should tell Hannah, who has come back looking more upset than before: She may learn to live without, but the need doesn't go away. She will always be in want of a mother.

———

In the morning I take my time in the bathroom, examining my face and body. I have not been sleeping well. Donato texts after everyone has gone to bed. *Come to me*, he teases, because he knows that I won't.

I need to dye my hair again; my roots are already beginning to show. I remember once Emily and I were doing our nails on the beach, and she said, *I wonder how many more times I will have to cut them.* Such a sad thing for a kid to think about.

I can hear the commotion of plates and silverware and Italian chatter coming from the breakfast room, which is beneath the main house. I imagine Paul, Marie, and Tonio are down there. Tonio has arranged a tour of Egnazia, an archaeological park that will feature in their book. He wants everyone to go, but I know Hannah will try to get out of it. Donato said she followed him inside to ask if they could go into town alone. *What can I do?* he asked, shoulders raised. *I had to say no.*

My patience with my niece is starting to wear thin. After dinner she moped on the walk back to the *masseria*. Paul had to stop several times to wait for her. *Keep up*, I called, but she did not respond. She never asked about my ankle either, which is scratched and bruised from when she pushed me off the *faraglione*. I can tell she means to go on like this, slowly transforming into the disconsolate teen that Emily became. *Stop mothering me, just stop!*

When I come downstairs everyone's *buongiorno*s echo on the tufa walls. It's a cavernous space, carved directly into the rock. Skylights fill it with gentle light. Donato is sitting with Hannah and his mother, Tonio and Paul are loading their plates from the sideboard.

"You have to try this omelet," Paul tells me.

There are cakes and cookies, yogurts and homemade jams, an array of dried meats and cheeses. I take a kiwi from a bowl, and two tiny apricots, one of which, I realize after I bite into it, is bruised.

Hannah pouts. "But I want to go to the beach again."

"You can go later," Paul tells her.

Agostina brings out a ceramic pitcher full of hot coffee. "Apulia is more than its beaches," she says.

"Why did we come here if you aren't planning to go to the beach once?"

He blinks at his daughter. "But you've gone almost every day."

"*You* haven't, and I want to go again." She crosses her arms. "Cilla and I were planning to buy snorkeling gear, weren't we?"

I take a piece of omelet from her plate. "Oh, that is good, Agostina, what's in it?"

She smiles. *Un segreto.*

"Wouldn't you rather go to the beach than to see another ruin?" Hannah tries again.

"Actually, I'm a little sunburned."

She narrows her eyes. "Then Donato can take me," she says, looking at him.

"*Cucciola mia,*" Marie says, laughing lightly. "I have barely seen my son. You will like Egnazia, it is right on the coast. We can walk to the beach afterward."

Hannah looks at her plate. Her nostrils flare slightly, just like Emily's would have.

"An old student of mine is giving us the tour," Tonio tells me, looking very pleased with himself. "I helped him get the position."

Paul leans in. "The necropolis is a smorgasbord of changing burial rites, built almost on top of each other."

"I don't want to see any more stupid ruins!" Hannah jumps up from the table, sending the ceramic pitcher crashing to the floor.

"Hannah," Paul shouts. "Look what you've done."

My niece's face is pink. "Why can't you talk about anything else? Don't you think there's enough death around us? Don't you think we see it all the time?"

Marie tries to take her arm but she pulls away.

"I refuse to go." She stomps a foot. There are tears now, and when she looks at Donato she chokes back a sob and rushes from the room.

"I'll talk to her," I say, but Paul stops me. Agostina is already cleaning the spilled coffee and bits of broken ceramic.

"She can stay here," he says. "It'll do her good to be on her own. She can think about how she's been behaving."

The ruins of Egnazia are on the wrong side of the highway to be considered seaside. It's more seaside-adjacent. They're different from any that I saw in Rome, maybe because the Forum and the Colosseum had a city bustling around them. There are no wailing ambulance or police sirens here. No music from street performers, no bus exhaust or diesel fumes. Only the smell and sound of the sea and the stone foundations where a city once stood, knobs of columns still crumbling. The valley stretching out on either side. The wind increases, pulling at the weeds and flowers and short scrub brush. It is shockingly bare. The kind of emptiness made louder because there had once been something here.

Tonio's colleague is waiting for us inside the museum, which is quiet except for the hum of the air-conditioning. He shakes hands with Tonio, looking respectful and eager. It's clear the tour is meant for him and Paul—and Donato too, since he is Tonio's son. It isn't long before he's no longer speaking in English. Marie translates as we go from display case to display case. Gradually, though, I realize she's not reading the labels or listening to our tour guide; she doesn't have to. She knows this information as well as her husband, who has moved on with the others to the next room.

"These are findings from female burials," she tells me. "Mostly objects associated with women's work."

She points out loom weights and spindles, jewelry, makeup containers made out of shells.

"There were not many jobs for *ancient* women," she says.

"I think you mean women of the ancient world, but you're right either way." We both laugh even though I don't see any gray in her hair.

"What's this?" I say, pointing to a large vessel.

"*Enchytrismoi*," she says sadly. "Containers to bury dead children."

She presses a finger against the glass. "Do you see the toys shaped like animals? There would be a bell inside, like toys today, no? They were buried with the child."

In the overhead lighting we watch dust float beside them.

Marie sighs. "Most babies did not survive to adulthood."

"Are you okay?" I ask.

"I would have liked more children, but Tonio . . ." She sighs again. "What about you? You're so good with Hannah, you did not want children of your own?"

Another question I don't have an answer for. A different kind of fear, a certain type of tiredness. I want to point at the primitive toy horses and crushed baby bottles and the ruins around us and ask how anyone can want children. And besides, what was I to Emily? And later to my dad as he got sicker and sicker, and now to my own mother? Maybe in another language, an ancient one, there is a word for motherhood that makes space for me. That includes what I am.

"It was never the right time," I tell her.

Outside, the men are waiting for us at the entrance to the excavated necropolis. From this angle Egnazia looks like ruins from nineteenth-century landscape paintings. Emily and Paul had prints like it framed in their living room. I remember the peach and purples—a sheep herder in the foreground, and the ruins in shadow, or jutting up into the sky, refusing to collapse. They had been wedding presents, I think. From Emily to Paul.

We descend a short flight of stairs into a multiroomed tomb, Marie translating for me.

"He is saying females are found with pomegranates and

bones from sacrificed piglets—there is a link between women and the fertility of the land." She points to letters carved into the rock. "*Tabara Damatria*. Priestess of Demeter, this is her tomb."

I can hear the wind above us, moaning across the ruins. There are many more tombs, each empty and dark. I can understand why Hannah did not want to come. There is a limit to how much death a person can bear witness to. I shiver even though it's muggy and there is sweat at the back of my neck. Donato is ahead of me, standing with his father and Paul. He turns then, smiling at his mother—or me, or maybe both of us.

"Do you think it's okay if I go back?" I ask.

Marie has wrapped her arms around herself. "Do you want me to go with you?"

I shake my head. "No, you enjoy the tour."

She hands me a map from the museum. I hear Paul ask where I'm going, and Marie answer in Italian. I walk quickly in case he's decided to follow. The wind is gusting again, blowing in great tufts. I can hear it in my ears, a *boom-boom-booming*. I watch it shake the tops of the olive trees, bending the sparse grass along the ancient walls.

Other tourists are wandering among the ruins now. Their polos and khakis, their pastel vacation clothes, cameras around their necks, those sun hats and visors—they comfort me. Clothes for the living. I turn toward the sun, try to feel its warmth, but the wind is blistering, kicking up dust and dirt from the highway, sending leaf litter across the ruins. I watch the tourists shield themselves from the sudden assault and then retreat into the museum or the necropolis.

Signs of mortality are everywhere—in the overturned bricks, the broken mosaic floors, the remnants of an amphitheater. Here is the road Trajan built; there, a furnace for a kiln;

what might or might not have been a basilica or two. A whole city. Gone. Something presses into me, a heavy burden.

I've climbed over a short wall and found a hidden out-of-the-way corner, beneath a large olive tree. Swifts swoop across the sky. There must be twenty of them, all diving and soaring against the wind. My eyes sting, the tears seem dried up.

"Cilla," comes Donato's voice. I don't think I've ever been so happy to see his beautiful boyish face. Maybe this is why people have children. He hops over the wall and crouches beside me. "You aren't supposed to be over here, did you not see the sign?"

I wipe at my eyes. "I can't read Italian. Do you have a cigarette?"

He takes the unlit one from behind his ear and hands it to me, leaning over to light it.

"Thank you," I say, inhaling deeply.

We watch the swifts for a moment, calling to one another. It's a sharp and urgent sound.

"What is Cilla thinking?"

I rub the cigarette out. *I don't want to think of anything.* It could have been a reflex—grabbing his hand and placing it on my breast, pinching the nipple between his fingers so that I cry out. As natural as breathing. I cannot look at him; his mouth is open in shock. I shut my eyes.

"Cilla." I hear the alarm in his voice.

I guide his hand to where I want to feel his fingers most. I push against him. I can hear myself, a feminine throaty sound, and I can smell the dry grass, the pungent sea. It's strange to accept that I could live a thousand lives and still it would not be sufficient. All that there is, is not enough—but I had known this already.

When I come, it's like a jolt. I imagine this is why the swifts have moved on, flown off for the safety of the sea cliffs. Why the cicadas suddenly seem louder, why Donato is looking at me with something like awe.

———

Agostina rushes toward us in the *masseria*'s car park, frantic.

Food poisoning, Donato translates for me. Hannah is very sick. Paul follows Agostina in search of medicine, a fresh set of sheets and towels, ice water—anything to make his daughter more comfortable. After the tour at Egnazia he had been lax to leave, almost accompanying Tonio and the former student to a late lunch, but then deciding at the last minute to return with Marie, Donato, and me. *Hannah is not answering her phone*, he had said sheepishly. *I should check on her.*

"She wants you," Paul says to me as he comes out of Hannah's room. "Agostina's phoning to see if any pharmacies are open this late."

Hannah's room is much more modest than mine. There's no sitting room, only a bedroom and adjoining bath. She's drawn the curtains so that it's nearly dark. And it's warm, stuffy. The fan on the ceiling circles, the A/C turned down low.

"She has chills," Paul says to me.

I watch her eyelids flutter. "Maybe it's the flu?"

He raises his hands. "Agostina doesn't have a thermometer." He looks as if he might cry.

I retreat to the window, where the air doesn't feel so full with the stench of vomit.

"She's going to be okay, Paul."

I try to open it because there's another, indescribable smell in the room. *Sickness*. A smell I know well. Not just with Mom, but toward the end, when Dad was in and out of the hospital with pneumonia.

His body is giving up, Emily would say. *Death is a part of life*. Such an easy platitude. Like *he'll always be with you*, or *she's watching down from heaven*. But she was on the outside looking in, phoning or texting instead of coming by the hospital. She wasn't accustomed to medicine charts and bathing rituals— she never had to cross that line between parent and child, when helping a nurse with a condom catheter was on par with cleaning his urine out of the bathroom rug.

"My head hurts, my whole body hurts," my niece groans.

"Hannah, sweetheart," Paul says, taking her hand. "I'm here. What do you want? What can we get you? Cilla's here too."

"Cilla's room," she says in a small voice. "Her bed is bigger."

"Sure, love, of course," he says, helping her out of bed.

"Will you bring my phone charger?" Hannah says to me.

I follow them into my room, which has been cleaned. The bed is neatly made, everything cool and calm. A breeze comes in through the open window. I watch the bougainvillea and palms in the courtyard bend and sway.

Hannah pulls down the blankets, pushing the pillows to the floor. She takes my robe, which had been folded and placed on the bedside table, and wraps it around herself.

"Oh, sweetheart, I'm sorry we left you alone." He kisses her head.

I know I should go to my niece, maybe sit on the end of the bed, stroke and pet her. She is hurting, she is sick. But I'm rooted to the spot. The stench has followed her, it clings to her clammy face, her oily hair. I do not want to play nurse. And I'm annoyed by how casually she usurped my things, how easy it was for her to think she could take what was mine. I move closer to the open window. I breathe in, try to remember that moment—Donato's surprise. His fingers still pressing against me.

"I feel awful," Hannah moans. "Will you shut that window? It's so hot out."

"Let me see if Agostina has left yet," Paul says, getting up. "I want to ask if she can get peppermint tea. That always helped when you were little and had a tummy ache." *Peppermint tea*, I hear him repeat to himself as he walks out of the room.

"How were the ruins?" she asks when we're alone.

I watch a lizard sunning itself on the stacked stone wall.

"It was fine," I tell her. "You were missed."

My niece sighs. "If you've seen one ruin, then you've seen them all. I hate that I cried in front of Donato. He always says I act like a child."

There is an image that haunts me more than the others. It was after we moved Dad to the rehab center to recuperate from that endless bout of pneumonia. His gums had started to bleed, and he was prescribed a mouthwash that cleaned his teeth so he didn't have to brush. I was holding one of those cheap plastic basins the color of chewed bubble gum up to his mouth, waiting for him to spit. How he kept on swishing, back and forth, back and forth—and it felt like such a long time that I finally said, *Spit it out, already*. And the look he gave me. It was as if I had asked him to hurry up and die, which in a way I had.

There's a knock at the door. Marie pops her head in. "May I see how the patient is?"

After Donato and I rejoined them at Egnazia I thought for a moment that maybe she suspected. I could not meet her gaze. *There you are*, she said to us. Donato had a deep flush beneath his tanned cheeks. She spoke to him in Italian, resting her palm on his forehead. But now she comes into the room and touches my arm gently before tending to Hannah.

"Is Donato here?" my niece asks.

"He's in the courtyard with Agostina and your *papà*. They're going to get you medicine." She speaks endearments in Italian, rubbing Hannah's back in a soothing rhythmic motion. "You will be better tomorrow."

I feel the steady forward marching of time then. The date of my return flight, which had felt so far in the future when I first landed, looms closer, closer still. Every second, every blink and breath—like a conveyor belt, I can feel its ceaseless turning. That date will come and I will go through the motions—the cab ride to the airport, the boarding of the flight, the collecting of luggage when I land—and then it will be nursing homes and hospitals, but that, too, will end. Tomorrow, this week, or the next. Five years from now. Twenty. *Snap*. Gone.

From the window I see Donato sitting at the courtyard table with Agostina and Matteo. Every button on his shirt is undone except for one, and I'm watching the wind whip up the bottom of it. He must have jumped in the pool or taken a shower, because his hair is damp and combed. Behind me Paul has returned, sitting on the end of the bed. "Is there anything else we can get you?" he asks, and I hear Hannah considering, "Hmmmm . . ."

"I'll go into town," I say, turning to them.

Paul looks at me, surprised.

"You should be here with Hannah," I tell him. "And Agostina has Matteo with her. It makes sense that I go."

Hannah frowns. "But you don't speak Italian."

"Donato can take me." I try to keep my face blank and sincere. It must work, because Marie goes on caressing Hannah's back, Paul nodding.

"But I want Cilla to stay here with me," my niece moans.

"I'll get the list from Agostina," I say over my shoulder. I catch Paul kissing his daughter's forehead, right where it is perspiring most. The nausea rises like a wave.

"Is she very sick?" Donato asks as he starts the car and we pull onto the shale road.

"She's fine." I roll down my window, breathing in that warm fragrant air. I want to tell him I've seen real illness, that I've been in the room with death, watched the final rattling breath, felt the pulse fade. But when I look at him, shirt blown open, changing gears with such brash confidence, I'm afraid I'd take something precious from him. Something I wouldn't be able to reconcile.

A train whistles in the distance. I think I can feel each and every rock beneath the tires. When we turn onto the main highway their vibration disappears, replaced with smoothness and acceleration. The olive groves become green smears on either side of us. There it is again, the drag and pull of it. The light is changing, the sun is starting to set. Like a current, dragging me out to sea. Every bump in the road is another moment gone.

Donato slows as we come into Fasano, where traffic becomes more condensed, the stoplights less reliable. At the pharmacy we wait in line. It's small and packed with various ointments and salves, deodorants and toothpastes. There are boxes of tampons stacked on the shelves, collecting dust, which seems appropriate. Donato buys tea and painkillers, and antinausea medicine.

But then something catches my eye, sends a shock right through me. "And this." I place the vaginal lube on the counter. I can feel Donato looking at me.

On the drive back, he pulls onto a dirt road and I slip off my underwear thinking about those ocean tombs. At Egnazia,

Paul had wanted us to see the part of the city that had sunk into the Adriatic. *We've come all this way*, he reasoned. We trekked a bit farther, to the nearby beach club, and hiked past the rows of white umbrellas and recliners where men and women were lying out, their skin oily and shining. Then down on the rocks the air suddenly turned rank. *What is that smell?* I asked. And he pointed to long rectangular holes cut into the rock, filled with dark water, a yellowish film on the surface. *Tombs*, he said. *This used to be the burial ground*.

"Come here," I tell Donato, and climb into the backseat.

Standing at the base of those watery graves, listening to the crowd at the beach club—when the wind shifted, I could smell their sunscreen and cigarettes. *If we had snorkeling equipment*, Tonio had said, *we could see it better.* I wondered what it would look like beneath the choppy waves, if it would feel different swimming there than in any other ocean.

The car is compact, but we make it work, and it's not until we're back at the *masseria* and I see Paul's bewildered face, and Tonio frowning, asking his son, "Why does Hannah think you're her boyfriend?"—that I feel Donato's semen leak out of me and seep down my leg.

—

Glasses of wine sit untouched on the courtyard table next to half-eaten focaccia. Tonio and Paul are silent, not looking at each other, while Marie continues to fuss over her son. I'm watching moths bump into the lanterns, a pair of bats flit above us in the night sky.

It keeps replaying in my head. Tonio's scowl, Paul and Marie standing behind him, waiting for an explanation. *I haven't done anything*, Donato had said, looking at me for confirmation.

I looked away because I could feel that wetness drying between my legs. *You kissed?* Donato's guilty half smile, his flustered laugh. *Who would not kiss a pretty girl? It was nothing.* I excused myself to take the medications to Agostina, who was watching over Hannah as she slept. *She's doing much better*, she assured me. *Amore, amore*, Marie was saying to her son when I came back out. Trying to soothe his embarrassment and guilt.

I keep my eyes on the moths, watch how they throw themselves at the light. The sound is loud, like a tennis ball hitting a wall.

Paul shakes his head. "What else don't I know?"

"Hannah's never had a boyfriend," I blurt out. "And she still doesn't have one." My voice is sharper and louder than it needs to be. I clear my throat. "Donato is a flirt. He flirts with everyone, even me. And Hannah is at an impressionable age. I think it's just a misunderstanding."

This is the best I can do, I reason. I'm tired. I wish I'd been the one with food poisoning. Although no one fusses over adult women when they have temporary illnesses.

Donato is still chewing at his nails. When he finally meets my eyes he gives me a sheepish grin, a childish shrug. It's the first time that I think maybe I dislike him.

"My poor little girl," Paul says, rubbing his face. "She's going to be heartbroken."

Marie clicks her tongue. "Donato, do you like her, *cuore mio*? You must if you kissed her."

"Hannah is a lovely girl, but we were just having fun."

"This isn't some girl you won't see again," Tonio lectures. "She is Paul's daughter."

Per favore, per favore, Marie attempts to placate them both. The three of them speaking in Italian.

What I want is to be in the backseat of the rental car,

occupying that moment—parked off a dirt road, windows rolled down, smelling the sea and the just-tilled fields. Could that have been with this same Donato, whose mother licks her finger to wipe a smudge from his cheek? Some other life, maybe, an absurd fever dream.

Marie is the only one talking now, her Italian even-keeled and soothing. The other three have their arms crossed but I can tell they are considering whatever it is she is proposing. When she's done speaking she waves her hand as if it were settled.

"I'm so tired," I tell them. "I have to get some sleep."

Marie is the only one to wish me *buonanotte*.

In Hannah's room, Agostina has changed the sheets and left the window open to air out the smell, but the pillows still reek of her hair, her toiletries are scattered about the bathroom. Shampoo and conditioner and face wash in the shower; a toothbrush and facial creams and a bag of makeup on the sink. Her suitcase is open on a chair, her orange bikini is drying on the window ledge. My niece has been with me every day and yet this is the first time I'm truly afraid she might find out about Donato and me. In a room filled with her things and her scent but empty of her. It was the same after Dad died. I sat in his office surrounded by his collection of colored glass, the late afternoon light making the room glitter. Majolica and transferware pottery, Vaseline and carnival glass. It wasn't his absence, but the impression he left behind. For a moment I had a sense of what I had lost.

I shower and try to sleep, but it's hopeless. The bed is narrow and the mattress is lumpy, and every time I close my eyes I remember the faint sounds Donato made in the car, between a grunt and a moan—and my own cries, or when Donato tried to cover my mouth and I tasted the palm of his hand.

I rinse a second time. When I'm drying off, I hear faint knocking. The door sticks and I have to force it from the frame.

"Donato," I whisper. "What are you doing?" The night air blows open the bottom of my robe. There are cicadas and an owl calling. I look down the passageway at the other closed doors.

"They've all gone to bed. Let me in."

He's shirtless, wearing only cutoff jeans. When he pushes past he lights a cigarette and goes to the window. "You did not answer my texts."

"Shh, keep your voice down. If anyone hears you . . ." I tie my robe tighter, which he notices.

"Suddenly you are shy?" He tries to pull me closer, but I move away.

I keep telling myself no one is awake, but every sound I think might be Agostina walking with Matteo because he can't sleep. Or maybe Hannah is sick again and needs me, or Paul saw Donato come into my room and wants to know why.

"I'm tired," I whisper. He tries to kiss me. "Donato, no."

"Why no?" He rubs his face. In the faint light coming from the window I can make out the fine blond hairs above his lip. He is trying to grow a mustache.

"You must have realized that Hannah liked you."

He shrugs his shoulders, that same guilty half smile on his face.

"Then why did you go on flirting with her—why did you buy her a necklace chain?"

He makes a motion with his hand. "That trinket? It was from one of those street vendors in San Lorenzo."

He lies down on the bed, pretending to inspect it. "Bigger than the back of the car." He grins.

"Your parents are one room over," I remind him. "And Paul is right next door."

"That has not stopped us before." He stretches out, putting his arms behind his head. His naked torso distresses me. The scarce dark hairs at the center, his broad shoulders and narrow waist—all signs of youth in bloom. I'm remembering the sound of his teeth grinding, and how, when he comes, he holds his breath as if he were jumping into water. A puff of air when he surfaces.

"You're deleting our text messages, right?"

"Of course," he says. *"Vieni qui." Come here.* His hand disappears beneath his shorts.

"Did you hear that?" I go to the window. The table and chairs where we sat hours earlier are pale in the moonlight. A gust of wind pulls at the pines, shaking their spindly branches; needles scurry across the stone bricks.

"You have to go," I tell him, pulling him from the bed. He wants a kiss, refuses to leave until I've given in. It's short and sloppy, and tastes of something far more noxious than cigarettes.

———

"Buongiorno!" Hannah cries, bounding down the stairs and into the breakfast room, where the rest of us are eating.

Marie stops chattering with her son and Tonio. Paul puts down his fork. The only movement is from the steam on my Americano. All eyes are on Donato as he stands to pull out her chair.

"Brava!" Marie says to me, pressing her hands together.

I have to look away. It's entirely too much. The mother urging it along, the two fathers watching from afar, one unsure and nervous, the other aloof. If this were on television I would change the goddamn channel.

Papa overreacted, Hannah had told me. *I only said that a good boyfriend would check on his girlfriend—he pressed me about it and I was so sick at the time, everything came tumbling out.* I had tried to explain to her, *Your parents are good friends and colleagues, there is a lot at stake.* But she only wanted to hear Donato's reaction. *What did he say?* And when I repeated his words my niece stretched out in bed, kicking her feet and arms. *He said I was lovely?* And giggled and giggled. *If you keep acting like this*, I threatened, *you're well enough to get out of bed.*

I took charge of my niece's care. Motion for my limbs, activity for my brain. Anything to keep me occupied because every time I came out of Hannah's room there was Donato. *Why are you ignoring me?* he demanded, but then one of the girls who helps Agostina was coming across the courtyard with the laundry and we had to break apart.

I did not have an answer for him—except that whenever I stop moving, I remember his hands digging into my hips. Those long, knobby fingers, the rough wide flat palms—so misleading when the rest of him is boyish.

Or his delicate clavicle, like a wishbone. The feeling of touching his soft skin. *What kind of lotion do you use?* I asked once, and he laughed as if it were a ridiculous question. *I do not even use sunscreen*, he said. I picture him lying down in the backseat of the car, how I could hear sirens somewhere far off, whining—*polizia, polizia, polizia.* But I did not care.

No matter where I start, it ends with his moans, the string of Italian words he sometimes murmurs. Like a funnel, around and around and then his hands are on my hips, or he's in my mouth, and I hear him. It is a different kind of haunting.

"Isn't that a pretty sight?" Marie says, smiling at Hannah

and Donato. "They do look nice together." She might rebuke her son, but even when he's done something questionable like leading a friend's young daughter on, there is still a kind of un-assailable pride.

"Can Donato and I go to the beach after breakfast?" Hannah asks.

For some reason, everyone looks at me. I concentrate on slicing a kiwi in half, scooping the meat out with my spoon because I don't want them to see how pissed off I am. Of course, it would fall to me. Never mind that they aren't my children. I'll be the moral compass, the arbiter during this ridiculous charade. What outcome do they expect?

"You're only just feeling better," I say, gouging the kiwi.

"You are a little pale," Paul says, throwing a quick glance at Tonio, who does not look up from his book. "And I don't know if it's appropriate."

Donato is chewing on the end of his finger again. "Cilla, you can come with us."

I scrape the inside of the kiwi with my spoon, hollowing it out. I press so hard I tear its delicate skin.

My niece frowns. "We don't need a chaperone."

"What about a walk?" Marie tries. "You could take the path in the olive groves."

I can tell Donato is frustrated, but he's obedient, and after he and Hannah are done with breakfast he follows her outside.

Marie leans forward in her chair after they're gone. "I am not entirely surprised, I even suspected."

I know what she's doing. She's looking for someone to be on her side. The harmonious threesome has been disrupted. I can tell by their body language. A chair between Paul and To-nio, a table separating Marie from them both. The space might as well be infinite. Nothing changes adult relationships quicker than when their children are involved.

I start on a second kiwi. The poor fruit.

Paul is running a hand over his face. "Well it's taken me completely by surprise."

He looks tired, there are dark circles under his eyes. *Should we take Hannah to a hospital?* he had asked. *She'll be okay*, I assured him. Emily had food poisoning once, and it was exactly the same. Several hours of being violently ill, then she spent the next day in bed while I made her soup and brought her Vitaminwater. I don't remember where our parents were, but afterward, our mom apologized to us, saying, *It wouldn't have been a good time to get sick, it's pilot season, you understand.*

"They make a good match," Marie tries again.

I somehow keep from rolling my eyes. Tonio snaps his book shut and leaves without saying a word.

Paul hesitates, examining his empty mug. "I'm not very comfortable with any of this."

"*Amore*, Donato will fix everything. He is taking this seriously," Marie says, touching his arm. "He has promised to be the perfect gentleman. Let it run its course, it will work out."

"They shouldn't be vacationing together, right?"

"She's in the main house now," Marie reassures him. "Agostina has switched Cilla's and Hannah's things, they're separated."

"You've done too much, Cilla," he says, covering my hand with his. It's shocking to feel the warmth of his skin. It takes the anger right out of me. I'm worried he can see the guilt in my face.

"It's really fine," I tell him, sliding my hand away. I'm remembering when Hannah was tucked in bed, how she was texting her friends and saying, *They're soooo jealous. Trish and Tina can't believe it, oh I wish I could see Silvia's face.* When I came out of her room there was Donato. He tried to tell me his plan to break it off with her. *When we get back to Rome . . .* But I stopped him. It would be an additional betrayal to know.

———

Lizards scurry as I approach the recliners by the pool. I lay out my towel, brushing away the large black ants.

Respond to one, I tell myself as I sign into my e-mail. Pick any of them. The cicadas are piercing. It's sweltering in the shade.

The real estate broker has written to suggest that I replace the fence, which is collapsing under the weight of overgrown honeysuckle. He's included numbers for several contractors. I can hear our mom's voice telling us, *Something to mark the occasion, of your and your sister's births.* It is actually two plants, grown into one.

I open another e-mail. *Where are you? I don't expect much, but the least my daughter can do is e-mail . . .* I click that closed too. There are messages from Guy; the roofer and exterminator are still waiting for replies. And then there are the junk e-mails: a price alert for fares from Los Angeles to Rome; a backlog of weekly news briefings from *The New York Times*; Macy's is having a sale. I shut my laptop and slide it away from me.

My forehead is freckled with sweat. I imagine Donato's and Hannah's ice creams are melting before they've had a chance to eat them. Paul suggested a trip into town after lunch, Hannah was enthusiastic until she realized he meant to go with them.

If I close my eyes, I can shut it all out. The e-mails, home, that looming return flight. There is only the pealing of the cicadas, the heat pressing into me like a weight—but then there is Donato on the train, in the olive groves, at Egnazia. My chest is tight, I'm about to cry.

"Okay if we join you?" Marie calls from the pool gate. She's with Matteo and a man I haven't seen before. He's maybe my age, with a shaved head and clad in board shorts and a sports jersey.

"Matteo's *papà*," Marie says, laying her towel beside mine. She hands me an arm floatie to inflate. *Matteo, Matteo*, she sings as she rubs sunscreen into his skin. I've forgotten how heady the smell of a baby can be. Especially on a hot day. It overpowers everything.

Matteo's dad nods as he pulls off his jersey. He's stocky and muscular and heavily tattooed. A gold chain and pinky ring glint in the sun. He swims to the side of the pool where we are, speaking Italian to Marie. I recognize the word *zia*.

Now that he's closer I'm not sure how old he is. He looks as if he's spent his entire life in the sun, his skin is creased and red. He could be thirty or fifty. When he smiles, I notice a gold eyetooth, polished and shining. He has very bright blue eyes, just like his son.

"How do you like Apulia?" he says in a thick accent. "Different from Malibu?"

Malibu, sounds like *malleable*.

"Gorgeous," I tell him. "The beaches here—*bellissima*."

He's making faces at his son, who's turned toward him.

"You cannot buy beer on Malibu beaches," he says.

Matteo stands on the edge of the pool, and Marie and I encourage him, clapping and shouting his name. "*Bravo!*" we cry when he makes the leap into his father's arms.

"He is a fisherman, and gone a lot," Marie says. We're watching them play together in the pool. "But he is very good with Matteo."

"Where's Tonio?" I ask.

"Reading in his room. He is worried about Hannah and Donato. I tell him it's okay, but—" She sighs.

"*Uno, due, tre.*" Matteo's dad is tossing the boy into the air and then catching him. Matteo shrieks with delight.

"Did I interrupt your e-mails?" She's taken off her cover-up and is rubbing sunscreen into her skin in the same slow luxurious movements as when we were at the spa together. I wonder if this is how she applies all lotions, or if this is for show. I catch Matteo's dad peeking over. She isn't wearing a bikini, but a black-and-white one-piece that ties across her back like a corset.

"Would you mind?" She hands me the sunscreen and turns away. Her skin is looser than I thought it would be, almost like a sponge. But there are no blemishes, not a freckle or a mole.

"Did you get between the straps?"

I tell her yes, even though no, I did not. I don't want to go on touching her skin—and part of me wants her to get sunburned. To add a flaw, like a notch in a tree.

"Do you want me to rub some on you?" she asks.

"No, no. I'm in the shade."

She shrugs and relaxes in her recliner. I can hear Matteo's dad blowing bubbles in the water. He laughs when his son tries to mimic him.

"I want to thank you," Marie starts. Her recliner is angled toward the pool; I can't see her face. "Paul and I, we want to do something nice for you. Would you like a *pumo di fiore*? They are good luck."

"You don't have to get me anything."

She twists so she can look at me. "I trust my son, but Hannah is young—and, *allora*, we take comfort in knowing you have been with them."

I'm thinking about when Donato was playing tour guide in Rome. He wanted to show me his favorite church, Hannah waited outside with the dog. The temperature dropped the moment we entered—gone were the crowds of tourists and hustlers and street performers. Only the smell of frankincense; and mosaic and marbled floors, ionic columns and chapels and domes, a Renaissance painted ceiling. I followed Donato, impressed by the painters and sculptors he could name, the dates and histories he could recite—and then Hannah was there.

It's so hot, she said. *I had to get out of the sun*. It was astonishing how much she looked like a teenage Emily. Fashionable and blond in a short linen jumper, hands on her hips, head tilted. A sour, spoiled expression on her face. I took a step back, worried she might direct her ire at me.

A uniformed guard appeared, pointing at Hannah's bare legs and shaking his head. She spat something in Italian that made his eyes go big, but then Donato was between them. I imagine he said, *Don't touch her*, or something like it because my niece looked satisfied. She went on yelling, though—their voices getting louder and louder. Families and couples and tour groups paused to watch. Nuns peeked out from the gift shop.

Shh, calm down, I said, but no one was listening.

Stupid Italian pigs! Prudes, all of you, Hannah was yelling. *It's the twenty-first century, a woman can wear whatever she wants!*

The security guard had Donato by the arm, he was using a two-way radio.

Look, look, I told the guard, waving my old studio ID in his face. I made a filming motion with my hands. *Hollywood*, I said. *We are scouting for a movie. These are my guides.*

The guard examined the ID and reluctantly let him go. And I remember outside how Hannah and Donato had laughed. Like two misbehaving children who got away with it.

Cilla, you sneak! my niece said. *Can you get me a studio ID?* I was about to lecture them, to play the role of adult, but then Donato was grinning that damn grin. *You were wonderful*, he said, and I could feel that heat in the center of me, how breathless I was because of it, and I didn't say or do anything.

"Where is that son of mine?" Marie says. "I thought they would be back by now."

"I think I'll take a dip." I get up and leave her to sunbathe alone. The rocks surrounding the pool are hot, I have to walk quickly. I hop the last two, which makes Matteo laugh.

"Did you think that was funny?" I smile, wading into the shallow saltwater pool. Matteo's dad is gliding him across the water in serene movements. He stops when I reach them.

"Matteo, practice English," his dad instructs.

"He doesn't have to. *Buongiorno*," I say, and lightly splash the surface, which makes Matteo laugh some more.

"He knows an English word." He speaks gruffly to Matteo, until he tries to pronounce *hello*, sounding more like *all-oo*.

"Very good!" I feel the strain in my smile. There is a twitch in my eye. "Are you ticklish?" I ask, and he squirms when I start to tickle his sides. He's splashing and giggling, and I tickle until he's gasping.

"*Basta, basta*," his father says, moving the child away from me. Matteo rubs his eyes. He might be crying, but it's hard to tell, and when I ask, he hides his face.

"Is he okay? Was I too rough?"

His dad makes a motion with his hand, speaking to me in Italian.

"I don't understand, I'm sorry."

He repeats himself, holding up his fingers. He might be saying, *You don't know Italian, not even a little?*

"Nope." I shake my head.

He laughs, which makes me laugh. "*Va bene*," he says. "*Va bene*."

I did not hear when Donato and Hannah arrived, but there they are sitting at the table with Marie, watching us. The expression on Donato's face makes me get out of the water and slip into my robe. Matteo's dad follows me with his son.

"How was ice cream?" I take one of the empty chairs across from them.

Marie wraps Matteo in a towel, and Matteo's dad, who has not bothered to dry off, sits beside me. Water drips onto my arm. "*Mi dispiace*," he says, wiping it with his hand. His skin is cool from being in the pool. I look away from Donato.

"It was nice," Hannah says. "Papa paid for it."

Matteo's dad says something in Italian, gesturing to Donato.

"I have a job." Donato frowns. He sniffs, adjusts the crisp corners of his collared shirt. "I'm social media manager for a club in Roma."

"He likes nice things, *amore*," Marie says, looking at her son. Matteo has fallen asleep on her shoulder, thumb in his mouth.

Matteo's dad laughs. I recognize the word *ragazzo* and the twitch of anger in Donato's face. It had been the same in the beach parking lot. A slight sneer, a tilting of his chin.

"Cilla, how was your afternoon?" Donato asks. He tucks a cigarette between his lips. "Did you have a nice swim?"

"Donato," his mother says, motioning to the child. "The smoke is bad for him."

He looks at Matteo's dad and lights the cigarette anyway. I don't have to speak the language to know he's being an ass. Matteo's dad says something in Italian, it's in a jovial, dismissive tone. He tousles Donato's hair when he walks past him, that gold eyetooth glinting, and takes his son from Marie.

"Ciao," he says to us as he heads back to the house. When he looks at Donato, he starts to chuckle again, shaking his head.

———

Agostina is calling to one of the girls who helps with breakfast. I can imagine the commotion in the kitchen. It was the same each morning. The clattering of dishes and glasses and silverware as they set up the sideboard and tables, Italian echoing off the cavernous walls, Matteo's gurgling laugh.

I pull the sheet over my head and turn onto my side. I have every intention of skipping breakfast; of not leaving the room until lunch and the little A/C unit becomes no match for the heat outside. I'm not interested in witnessing Hannah and Donato dine at the table set especially for the two of them. Paul and Marie and Tonio nearby, their dynamic now awkward and unsure. And if Matteo's dad is down there, Donato will try to humiliate him again. Last night, Matteo's dad grilled *arrosticini* for us, and Donato kept the conversation on Bernini and Caravaggio, Guercino and Tassi. He laughed that boyish heehaw when Matteo's dad tried to join in. *The Scrovegni Chapel is not Baroque*, Donato said, grinning at me. *You are thinking of Giotto.*

I reread his text from last night: *We play in the olive fields tonight, sì?* ♥

Sleeping has been difficult. I lie awake listening to the cicadas. It's a sound that, when focused on, starts to suffocate the body. I get up and pace around the room to keep from feeling pressed into the bed, as if dragged into something darker than sleep.

I texted him back, *Not tonight, be patient.* Every sound outside might have been Donato about to ask for admittance. A crack of sticks, the wind twisting the cypress trees. I relaxed only when the sky started to lighten, the horizon turning pale pink. It's a different type of sundowner. *The natural progression of things*, one of the nurses had said when Dad refused to sleep at night.

I delete both my text and Donato's. Someone starts to vacuum the room next door; the sound is oddly soothing. There is muffled chattering too. The amiable voices of shared work. I fall into a thick, syrupy sleep. The kind where I'm dreaming I'm awake, walking around the room. It's like quicksand—but then there is knocking and Paul's voice, "Hello? Cilla?"

"Yes." I struggle awake.

"Are you not feeling well? You missed breakfast."

The room is overly warm. "One minute," I shout, untangling myself from the sheets and pillows.

"There's a focaccia bakery in town," he says as I open the door. "I thought you might want to go with me since you haven't eaten yet."

I peer around him to the passageway, which is empty except for the maid's cart filled with cleaning supplies and toilet paper and boxes of tissues.

"Everyone's changing for the pool," he says. "We're taking a break from the book."

I change into a sundress and meet him in the courtyard, where Marie is lounging with Donato and Hannah.

"She lives!" Marie takes my hand. Her bathing suit straps peek from beneath her dress.

Donato is shirtless, wearing only swim trunks. His body looks much too long and brown and soft against the rough pinewood chair.

"You are going with Paul? We will come with you." For a moment he looks desperate, his eyes large and pleading.

"You ate an entire omelet at breakfast," Hannah says. A towel rests on the table in front of her. "I thought we were going to swim."

"We should get going," Paul says. "The article I read said they can sell out by eleven."

"No time to change, then," I tell Donato.

They follow us out to the car park, where Matteo's dad is playing with a soccer ball. He's wearing a blue-and-white striped jersey, his forehead and neck dripping.

"Ciao," he calls to us.

"It's hot out here," my niece replies, holding open the gate to the pool for Marie and Donato. "Come swim with us."

"Paul and I are going into town for focaccia," I tell him, though I don't think he understands. He bounces the ball from one thigh to the other.

Donato has stopped to watch him.

"Fo-ca-ccia," he says, tapping it out with each muscular leg.

"*C'è solo l'AS Roma*," Donato says, knocking the ball away from him.

Marie claps her hands together, Hannah leans on the wall. Paul even gets back out of the car to watch their scrimmage. Dust and dirt rise around them, loose shale grinds under their quick feet. I think I see Donato push Matteo's dad, but he's so big it must be like trying to budge stone. Donato is sweaty and panting, and when Matteo's dad lunges for the ball, Donato trips, and goes sliding against the ground.

A flurry of Italian endearments and concerns from Marie and Hannah as they run to him.

"Is he hurt?" I ask, remaining by the passenger door.

"*Basta, basta*," I hear Donato say to his mother and Hannah. "It is only a scratch."

"He's got some gravel in his palm," Hannah says, examining it.

Matteo's dad offers him a hand, but Donato ignores him.

"We should go," Paul says, looking at his watch. Donato follows his mom and Hannah back inside to ask Agostina for a first-aid kit. He does not look at me.

"Hopefully they haven't sold out," Paul says, starting the engine. "*The New York Times* said it's not to be missed."

The car bumps along the dirt road. He slows as we come to a roundabout, studying the GPS screen. We circle twice before he decides which way to go, and curses when he realizes he was wrong.

"I always read these damn things backward," he says, making a U-turn across the median. The driver behind us holds down their horn.

He chuckles when he notices I'm hanging on to the roof handle. "You remind me of your sister, she hated when I drove."

"I can see why," I say, which makes him laugh harder.

He slows as we come into town, braking hard when a pedestrian runs across the street. I brace myself against the dashboard. The focaccia place isn't anything special, but Paul takes his time choosing which loaf he wants, then chats with the workers as they ring him up.

"I had an ulterior motive when I asked you to come," he says, glancing at me as we climb into the car.

My chest is tight. I pretend to be preoccupied with the bag of bread, which is warm; oily spots have soaked through the paper.

"Does Hannah seem okay to you? I can't tell anymore."

I breathe out. "She's a typical teenager, boy crazy and emotional. Emily was a lot like her at that age."

He smiles. "It's hard to imagine Em like that. She was a different person when we got together."

The focaccia has made the car smell good, all fresh herbs

and yeast. I rip off a piece, the tomatoes burst, the salt seeps in. "This is delicious."

"Do you remember when you visited us in San Clemente?"

I nod, still chewing.

He smiles to himself. "She was so nervous, everything had to be perfect."

"Why? She worked the room, all eyes on her—as per usual." I've forgotten to mask my voice, Paul is taken aback. He looks at me from the corner of his eye.

"That's not how it was," he says, pulling into the roundabout again. This time he doesn't miss the turn. "Emily felt like the screw-up, pretty but not very bright."

"I wasn't the one who treated her like that—that was our parents, our mom, mostly."

"Then you can understand why she wanted you to see the life she'd made for herself. She was sober, she had intelligent friends that were doing things in the world. Did you know she was working on getting a degree?"

I shake my head.

"It was how she came to be at my NYU lecture. She had been going to all of the university's free public talks, trying to figure out what she wanted to study." He waits, trying to catch my eye. But I'm pretending to be distracted by the view out my window.

"She settled on history."

The same olive fields and crumbling farmhouses speed past.

I'm remembering something that I have not thought of in years, maybe decades. There was an El Niño the month I got my driver's license—streets were flooded, the north part of Pacific Coast Highway had closed from a mudslide. Mom and Dad were somewhere, a party, probably. They had forgotten to pick up Emily from her ballet practice. I remember being furious. It would have been the first time I'd driven myself to Guy's apartment. Like an adult—like a *real* woman. I had bought a new dress for the occasion. But just as I was about to leave the house, Emily called, and I had to cancel my plans.

Get in the damn car, I said to her when I pulled up. I intentionally swerved into puddles on the way home. Muddy water splashed the sides of the car, one so immense it covered the windshield, and I felt such a surge of recklessness that I laughed out loud. *Cilla, please, no more. You're scaring me*, my sister said. How pretty and delicate she looked in her leotard and raincoat. *One more*, I promised, and tried to cross a river of water and silt at the bottom of Corral Canyon. But the Land Rover stalled out, and we were stuck in the rain until we could flag down another car. Our mom was furious with me. *Your sister is soaked through.* I wasn't allowed to drive for a month—but the point is, Emily did not tell her what really happened. *We got lost*, she insisted. *It's not Cilla's fault.* I remember later asking why she lied. *Because.* She shrugged. *I understand why you did it.*

———

"Agostina's daughter has a drinking problem," Marie is saying, leaning in as if Paul and I were trusted confidants.

Ahead of us, Matteo is holding hands with his dad and grandmother—every few feet they count to three and swing him. The promenade is crowded; we had to park four blocks from the seaside restaurant where we're having dinner.

Uno, due, tre! And then Matteo's excited cries. The sky is a dusky blue beyond them.

"They moved back so Agostina can help with the baby."

"How sad," I say. When something drops out of Matteo's

pocket, Agostina squats to pick it up. I can make out a thong through her white jeans. What must it be like to be her daughter?

I hate how she treats you, Emily had said one holiday when our mom had gotten herself and Emily matching garnet earrings, and me a box set of Turner Classic Movies. *Doesn't it bother you?* she asked. I remember being more surprised by Emily's frustration than the gifts themselves. One of life's inevitable disappointments is the moment when a child sees their parent as a fallible human being, and for me, that had happened years before.

Paul turns to look at Donato and Hannah, who have stopped walking. "Are they okay?" he asks us.

My niece has her hands on her hips, Donato is shaking his head. His nose and forehead are badly sunburned. There is a Band-Aid on his palm from where he fell on it. He has spent the last two days lording over the pool as if it were his, scowling at Matteo and his dad whenever they came out to swim.

I'm fine, he said when his mother saw his face, and swatted away her hand.

"Stay together," Tonio shouts ahead of us. The streets are packed, ripe with body odor and cologne and cigarettes. I can feel heat radiating from the concrete walls and asphalt like precipitation evaporating. When we pass a gelateria, a group of boys take off on mopeds, sending puffs of black exhaust in their wake.

The restaurant is a sleek, recently remodeled place, with a fish tank and high-backed leather chairs, everything black and white.

Matteo's dad must know the waiter, because they embrace.

"Los Angeles," I hear him say, gesturing to me, and whatever else he says must impress him, because the waiter directs his attention to me. The menu recommendations and specials, his wine preferences—I'm the first glass he fills, and the only one for whom he unfolds the cloth napkin, placing it across my lap. "I have always wanted to go," he says in stilted English.

Donato, who had been sitting at the end of the table, excuses himself.

"He's very handsome," Marie says to me. "Maybe you can make him a Hollywood star!"

Hannah giggles. "I'd see anything he was in."

I think I can see Donato at the bar inside.

"With that mustache, he'd make a good porno star, no?" Agostina says, laughing at her own joke.

Donato comes out with a gin spritzer and drinks it fast— then, before the waiter can take our orders, asks for another.

"Agostina says the grilled octopus is the best in the Salento," Paul tells me.

Tonio signals the waiter over, asking about the octopus. Paul switches to Italian and then to English, asking if I think two orders is enough.

Donato sucks at his straw until he reaches the bottom. Then he wants to order a third.

"What about a glass of wine?" Hannah suggests.

"If I wanted wine, I would order wine," he says.

Marie pats his hand. "You drink too much, *cuore mio*."

He shrugs his mother off. "I can drink if I want to." He peers at me from over his glass, tilting it so he can crunch on the ice.

When my phone rings I'm relieved to step away from the table. Out in the street there's a warm wind coming from the ocean. Families and young couples drink at an outdoor bar with plastic chairs and tables, cigarette smoke wafting yellow under the fluorescent lights.

"Hello," I shout into the phone. My mom's doctor has to repeat himself.

"I'm having trouble hearing you," I say. "Hold on."

The bar has turned up its music. I can feel the bass vibrating through me, rattling my chest cavity. I walk away from it.

"What did you say?" I plug my other ear, trying to hear better. "I thought she was doing great, the physical therapist said she might be able to come home early."

He repeats himself, "Yes, but the episodes are escalating."

I don't realize I've walked to the beach until there is sand in my shoes. He's listing things now. "She also punched the night nurse."

"Was it the Russian one? She doesn't like—"

"Have you researched any long-term skilled nursing facilities? She will require a lot of care when she leaves here."

I swallow. "She can't stay there? I mean, now that she's worse?"

The line is quiet for a second and I think maybe I've dropped the call.

"We're a rehab center, Ms. Messing. Short-term only."

There's a metallic taste in my mouth now. I spit into the sand to get it out. He's talking about paperwork and specialists. He's telling me social services will be in touch.

"I haven't—I'm not in the country."

"When do you expect to be back?"

The most natural question in the world. I cannot forever be on vacation. The flight itinerary is printed, it reads late next week—but part of me, I realize, had hoped never.

A group of twenty-somethings passes by, barefoot and dressed in loose flowing dresses, casual linen pants, and panama hats. Their voices catch on the wind—a foreign language I don't recognize and can't understand. I watch them pad down the beach, toward the clubs, where neon lights flash across the water.

"Ms. Messing," he is saying, "I know this is difficult."

I feel myself recoil from the thought of having to do it all over again. The pill regimens, the grocery lists, the ordering of the medical equipment, the laundry and bathing.

I turn and see Donato making his way across the sand.

"I have to go," I tell the doctor. It's the first time I hear genuine alarm in his voice. "But Ms. Messing, Ms. Messing," he stammers.

I hang up just as Donato reaches me. He doesn't say anything, just pushes me against the breakwater. His hands are on my breasts, his tongue thrusts into my mouth. He tastes sour and leaden—and I'm thinking of that sterilized smell of medical equipment, how the cleaning solutions have that acerbic sweetness. Like store-bought diapers, like flowers past their bloom.

I push him off. "Donato, not now."

He says something entirely in Italian.

I grab his hand. "You're drunk."

"*Succhiami il cazzo.*" He dissolves into giggles. "Do you know what that means?"

He tries kissing me again, rubbing himself against my thigh. "You should, it is your favorite thing."

He kisses my neck, my chin. "You are good at it Cilla, *Zia* Cilla."

"Don't call me that."

He's undoing his pants, expecting that I will drop to my knees here in the sand.

Your mother wants to come home, the doctor had said. *But is that what you want? She will require full-time care.*

I don't think I have it in me, in fact I know I don't.

"I'm going back to the restaurant."

"*Che palle!* Why not? Why not when I want to?" He punches the breakwater.

I try to catch his fist before he slams it again, but he is sweating and slick.

"Don't do that! Your mother—"

I can feel blood from his cut-up knuckles smear on my skin. I'd forgotten that it isn't always the parent who disappoints. Sometimes it's the child—it must be both. Neither can be who the other imagines them to be.

"Where are you going?" Donato grabs for my hand but misses. He must swear in Italian, but it's hard to hear anything. The wind has intensified, muffling everything except for the beach clubs, their music still thumping.

———

I dream that my sister is so close I can smell her L'Occitane lotion, I could reach out and hug her but she's emaciated and frail, and I'm scared she might break.

Do you want to put a warm cloth on her face? someone had asked. *She knows you're here.* And how I went downstairs and watched cartoons with Hannah, waiting for someone to come and tell us.

But then my sister's off, running away from me as she had done in life. The sound of her bare feet slapping against the stone steps.

I follow her to that side of the property where the honeysuckle gushes over the fence. Butterflies and bees waft among its vines and blossoms. My sister, this beautiful stranger, plucks a flower. She pinches off the calyx, pulling the pistil until a bead of nectar forms. *This is what hummingbirds drink*, our mom had told us once. I remember worrying about that—how can anything live on such meager sustenance? They must spend their whole lives going from flower to flower, trying to fill up.

Do you want to say goodbye? someone asked because the mortuary was coming to collect the body—and Hannah, her eyes big and blank, as she came out of her mother's room. *There is my sister*, I remember telling myself, trying to feel the weight of it and failing. *Emily is dead*.

I don't recall who decided she would be cremated, but I remember that afterward her ashes were to be scattered in the Pacific. Only our mom kept putting it off, and then Tonio offered Paul the position in Rome. It was decided Emily would be divided. Paul arranged a small ceremony at Leo Carrillo State Beach—and the remaining ashes sit in a porcelain urn facing that large window in the living room, looking out at the sea.

I wake up parched and twisted in the sheets. I get a bottle of water from the mini fridge and open the window. The tufa rock walls, the courtyard, and the *masseria*'s travertine façade—everything is pale and blue.

Donato's last text is open on my phone. After everyone had gone to bed, he messaged, apologizing and asking if I would come to his room. I did not reply.

I swipe through photos from Puglia. There is one of Hannah on the beach where we swam out to the *faraglione*. She is posing on her towel, head propped up by her hand, pursing her lips at the camera. She looks so much like my sister, like a young version of our mother, too, that I want to cry.

Light glows pale around the window shutters. I change into my bathing suit and slip a pack of cigarettes into my robe pocket. The door sticks, but then there are only the shocks of bougainvillea and palms, trembling in the early morning light. I walk quickly to the pool. Water striders skate across its surface. I dive in, sending the mourning doves in the nearby brush scattering.

It feels good to be weightless, free from that pull of Earth's orbit. Maybe I can change my flight. Or cancel it altogether. When we return to Rome things could go back to how they were. I swim across the pool in one breath and when I surface it's with the hope that not everything is inevitable.

I hear the crunching of pebbles underfoot, and there is Matteo's dad, carrying pool-cleaning equipment. He grins when he sees me, the gold tooth stark in the pale morning light.

"*Buongiorno*," I say, and climb out of the water, wrapping my robe around me. The cicadas have started their noisy song. "I couldn't sleep."

He sets the equipment down and leans on the wall beside me. We look out at the pool, which is calm again, quiet and serene.

"Would you like one?" I offer him the pack. Now that he's near I can see the stubble on his head is white.

He lights mine and then his own. When he exhales he examines the cigarette, saying something in Italian.

"I'm sorry, I don't understand."

A breeze kicks up, bending the olive trees. I pull my robe tighter.

"It is cold, no?" he tries.

"Not very."

"You see thousand-year-old tree?"

I shake my head. The jays nesting in the rocks are hunting for insects. They hop about the grass, heads twitching left to right.

"Come," he says, holding out his arm to me. "One thousand years old."

The sun has risen, everywhere is swelling with morning sounds. Things scatter from beneath our feet. Animals rustle in the bushes and trees. I want to ask about snakes, but I'm

172

afraid he won't understand. In the distance, I hear the train whistle as it continues its slow push through the olive groves, heading farther into the Salento.

Twice Matteo's dad helps me over a stacked stone wall or crumbling fence. He has very rough hands—dockworker hands. I wonder what his life has been like, how he met Agostina's daughter. What would it be like to be with him? He's holding my hand again, because I've lost my balance in the thick mushy dirt. One of his fingers has gotten twisted in my bikini tie. I blush and awkwardly try to untangle him.

It's very ugly, this millennium-old tree. The trunk is large and bulbous, as if it had bubbled in places and then been petrified. It is so large the two of us cannot wrap our arms around it.

"It's gigantic," I say, and for some reason this makes Matteo's dad laugh. I say it again, throwing my arms in the air for exaggeration. *Gigantic.*

He takes my hand then, placing one of the tree's small dark olives in my palm. He motions for me to eat it. His eyes are such a dazzling bright blue that I ignore his mischievous grin. He is practically jumping up and down. I play along, examining the olive and sniffing it.

"*Mangiala,*" he coaxes.

It is unbelievably sour; my whole face puckers. He is already laughing.

"Disgusting, no?" he says, wiping his eyes.

"*Sì.*" I spit, and laugh with him.

"Cilla," Donato shouts, grabbing my arm. He looks as if he's been awake all night walking the olive groves, hoping I might appear. His knuckles are cut up and bruised from the night before. *I slipped on the rocks*, he told his mother when he finally returned to the restaurant. *Poverino*, she worried over him.

"What are you doing out here with him?" He says something in Italian at Matteo's dad, who has propped himself against the tree trunk, looking amused.

"Let go of me." I wrench free from his grip. "Nothing is going on. He was showing me their thousand-year-old tree. I tried one of its olives."

Donato's chest is heaving. His complexion is sallow beneath the sunburn, his lips knitted in a thin grimace.

"*Il ragazzo è innamorato*," Matteo's dad says, laughing. *The boy is in love.* When he walks past Donato, he pats his face, speaking Italian in that same condescending tone.

I keep Donato from following after him.

"What do you think you're doing?" I ask when it's only us and the cicadas.

"*Sticazzi.*" He shrugs. "Who does he think he is?"

"You can't keep acting like this."

He lights a cigarette, blowing out a plume of smoke. The morning heat has already intensified, and it makes his tobacco smoke heavy. My robe and bathing suit will reek of it. It's the first time I feel real panic—cold and suffocating. Maybe he has already told someone. I can see him bragging to one of his friends. If not, then it's only a matter of time.

"Donato . . ." I try to make my voice steady. "No one can know. Look at me and swear."

But he won't look at me. He just kicks the trunk of the ancient olive tree, breaking some of its rough bark, and takes off, jogging farther into the groves.

———

Hannah and Donato are fighting. I've missed what it's over, but I can tell by Donato's sullen expression that it could have been anything. He picks at his cornetto beside my niece, who does not look up from her bowl of fruit when I tell them *buongiorno*.

Nearby, Paul is thumbing through a newspaper, Tonio a book; both pretending not to notice the two sulking teens sitting one table over. Bowls of cereal sit untouched in front of them, a plate of half-eaten toast. There is an empty seat between them.

"Everyone is quiet this morning," I say, taking a slice of plum cake from the sideboard. The panic I felt earlier creeps in again, but then Paul pulls out a chair for me.

"What did I miss?" Marie asks when she comes into the breakfast room.

Tonio grumbles something in Italian, gesturing to my niece and Donato. I imagine he is thinking, *I knew this is how it would play out.*

Paul fidgets in his chair. Marie's knife and fork scrape against her plate. I hear the clock in the main hall chime above us. Tonio turns a page of his book.

There is a commotion at the top of the stairs, and each of us strains to look. Matteo appears, dressed in a Spider-Man costume. He clambers down each step, with his dad in tow. Instantly everyone is transformed. Donato sings a superhero theme song, Hannah wants Matteo to sit on her lap, Marie wants to make him a plate of food—even Tonio and Paul must smile when Matteo shows them a drawing he made.

"It is of his favorite cat," his dad tells me. *Micia.*

"Let's pretend he's ours," I hear my niece say to Donato, Matteo babbling on her lap.

"We should all go to the beach," Marie suggests, looking around the room. "It would do us good to be in the sun and swim in the sea."

"It's the weekend," Paul says. "The beaches will be crowded."

Matteo jumps from Hannah and runs to his dad, who lifts him high into the air.

"I know of a secret beach," his dad says. "*Il Luogo Solitario.*"

"The Lonely Place," Agostina translates. She's come out from the kitchen, carrying Americanos for Donato and me. "It's a long hike, very steep."

The two of them chat in Italian.

"Is it a *real* beach?" Hannah interrupts. "I don't want to lie out on rocks. I'm always bruised afterward."

"A sandy beach," Agostina says. Hannah sits up with interest. "And there are caves with early Christian frescoes."

"I'd put on sunscreen for that," my brother-in-law says, smiling.

"Do you know how early they are?" Tonio asks. "Never mind, don't tell us. It will be more fun to figure it out ourselves."

"How much of a hike is it?" I ask.

"I show you how to climb down," Matteo's dad says to me. "You swim out. The water—*è bellissima.*"

"Donato?" Marie calls to her son. "Will you come with us?"

Donato has given up on his cornetto. He's pushing a spoon around a bowl of yogurt without taking a bite. He looks at me, then shrugs.

"*Allora.*" Agostina claps. "I will pack a lunch."

We take two cars, and arrive at the cliffs past noon. The wind is gusting. It knocks the car door closed when I try to get out. Marie ties her hair into a knot to keep it from whipping her in the face. Hannah pulls her baseball cap low. It's decided that Matteo's dad will show us the way down and come back for our lunch. "It can be dangerous," he shouts over the wind. Agostina holds Matteo tight. Donato carries a stack of towels and an umbrella under each arm. When one drops, Matteo's dad is there to retrieve it, hoisting it over his shoulder like a rifle.

Seguimi, he motions to everyone. The trail is overgrown with scrubby brush, nearly leafless from the harsh wind. I shield my eyes from bursts of dirt and sand.

Behind me I hear Paul. "Did you put on sunscreen?" he shouts to his daughter, who is hiking in a bikini and shorts. His nose is white with zinc.

When we start to descend, the wind is abruptly silenced by the sheer rocky cliffs. Matteo's dad stays a few feet ahead. He climbs down, then turns to assist me. I'm struck again by how rough his hands are. I can feel where he's gripped me long after he's let go.

"Let's rest here," Marie says, fanning herself.

Tonio shifts his backpack that has his camera and journal and books from one shoulder to the other. He uses a handkerchief to wipe his brow.

Matteo's dad offers me his water bottle. *Grazie.* I shield my eyes to look where the others are. Paul helps Agostina with Matteo, handing him over the rocks like a bucket of water between firefighters, Hannah pointing where to step. Donato's fallen behind, I can only see the umbrella, bobbing as he descends. He shouts in Italian to us.

"What is he saying?" I ask.

Matteo's dad chuckles.

"Not to wait," Marie says and smiles. "My son is very stubborn."

The last stretch is almost vertical stairs, carved right into the rock. I keep close to Matteo's dad, who leaps the last few feet into the white sand. He turns, those blue eyes bright against his ruddy face.

"A sandy beach," he says. He wants me to repeat after him in Italian. *Spiaggia sabbiosa.*

"My pronunciation." I laugh. "It's hopeless."

He holds out his arms.

I catch a whiff of him when he lifts me—different from Donato, who smells like expensive Italian cigarettes and a beguiling musk, almost herbaceous. Or Guy, who is all mints and cigarillos and chic cologne. I do not realize how wobbly my legs are until I'm standing in the sand. I lean against the rocks while Matteo's dad helps the others from the stairs, Marie and Hannah giggling as he swings them into the sand. He takes Matteo from Agostina and lifts him onto his shoulders. Donato is still far behind.

"Should we wait for him?" Paul asks. Sunscreen streaks his stubble.

"Papa, your face," Hannah says, trying to wipe it.

Marie raises her hands. "He says not to."

In the cave Paul and Tonio marvel at the decaying frescoes, telling anyone who will listen about Turk invasions and Saracen slaughters—eight hundred, nine hundred, one thousand years ago.

The cove on the other side is completely untouched. We have the white sands and turquoise water to ourselves. The bleached rocky cliffs on either side shield us from the wind.

"*Cosi bella!*" Marie exclaims, removing her caftan and digging her feet into the hot sand.

Hannah is trying to talk to Donato, who has finally caught up.

She purses her lips, saying loudly, "Did you know this is a local cliff-jumping spot?" She points to a rocky outcrop. "Matteo's dad says he and his friends used to jump from there."

"*Mio dio*, no," Marie says. "That is ten, twelve meters!"

Matteo's dad is playing in the sand with his son, and says something to Marie that makes her laugh and swat his arm.

This, I think, upsets Donato more than anything. He stalks off, toward the caves.

My niece watches him until he's disappeared. "I'm going swimming," she says, stepping out of her shorts. She wants Matteo's dad to show her where to walk in.

"I'll come too," Paul says, following them out. He is pale where his shirt covered him, and not as sure-footed as them.

Tonio heckles him from the shore.

"He would not do any better," Marie says to me.

Tonio laughs. "I heard that."

Paul is knocked under by a large wave, and when he surfaces, hair wet, he's dog-paddling. "*Victory!*" he yells to us. Tonio whistles and claps. "*Bravo! Ben fatto!*"

When Matteo's dad comes in from the water, he towels off next to me. I look to see if Donato is watching from the cave, but I don't see him anywhere.

"Matteo is hungry," Agostina announces.

"I will get lunch," his dad says, pushing one of Matteo's toy trucks across the sand.

"I'll go with you," I tell him. "You'll need help with the cooler."

I think maybe I'll see Donato in the cave, brooding beneath the chipped image of Christ. But he isn't there. I remember that first time with him, on the train speeding through the center of Italy. A different Cilla, a different Donato.

Scaling the rocks is harder than the descent.

"I'm out of shape," I tell Matteo's dad when we reach the top, but he doesn't understand. The labored breathing, the sweating through my caftan—those things must translate, because he lifts the cooler out of the trunk and hands me a can of soda and a bag of chips.

"We rest," he says, sitting on the trunk of the car. I hoist myself up beside him and offer the chips. He takes my soda instead, grinning. The wind has calmed; scrubby pine trees shade us from the sun. A wild, spicy scent emanates from him.

"Do you wear cologne?" I try, but he only keeps grinning. "You don't understand, do you? That's probably a good thing, I'm not making any sense."

That gold tooth glinting. "I understand enough."

And then, suddenly, there is Donato—exhausted child, the sunburn on his face peeling. He is shouting in Italian, finger in Matteo's dad's face. He turns to me.

"You fuck anyone, *si*? *Si*?"

"Shush." I try to hush him. "*Shhh*."

"*Puttana*," he shouts.

Matteo's dad is confused at first, but then his eyes get very large and he looks at me with such candor I have to look away.

I feel my face redden. Donato is furious. He pushes Matteo's dad, making him stumble.

Then they're squared up—bulky muscle to lean youth. From afar it must look like a father lecturing a son. Donato pushes him again, and Matteo's dad has grabbed him by the shirt collar—and for a moment, I want to see it happen. His fist is pulled back and I want to see the bones in Donato's beautiful face break.

But Matteo's dad doesn't hit him. His fist wavers, and instead he flings Donato aside. He points at me, spits something ugly. I know it's ugly because I understand one of the words. *Carampana*. Hannah had used it at the beach club in Monopoli, about a group of women my age but with more makeup—inflated lips and breasts, and slinky, barely there bikinis. One of them smiled and called out to Donato when we walked by.

Carampana, Hannah had sneered. An old woman who tries to be young and sexy.

I want to explain, but what can I say? Matteo's dad already understands, it's why he lifts the cooler and starts to hike away. It's why he looks back at me with disgust.

"Why did you not come last night?" Donato is saying. His hands on my hips. The wind has returned full force, tugging at the cliff side.

"What have you done?" I point to where Matteo's dad has disappeared. "He will tell Agostina, and she will tell your mother, and then—it's all over."

"What does it matter." His hands are on my waist now. "Don't you love me?"

He tries to kiss me, and I let him. For a moment I think if I let it happen, maybe he won't tell anyone else. Maybe I can get out of this unscathed. But he tastes different, his hands are too soft and hot and desperate.

"Donato," I start. He thinks this is a lover's quarrel and we are going to make amends. His hands have slipped beneath my caftan, they are trying to find access.

"Donato, stop."

"I come to California," he says, muttering those same Italian phrases he said in restaurant bathrooms and olive groves, in the backseat of the car and on the train. "I will stay with you in your Malibu house."

I can feel him, hard against my leg. "Donato, enough. Stop!"

He slaps me then. A quick, effective swipe.

The wind has returned, blowing receipts and napkins that have escaped from the car. It whistles in the pine branches above us. Donato reaches out, and when I move away he drops to his knees and starts to cry. "*Mi dispiace*," he repeats over and over, holding on to me, his voice cracking. "*Cilla, oh, Cilla, perdon-ami, perdonami.*"

His sobbing is growing louder. Nothing I say will quiet him, and he's speaking entirely in Italian. I can make out only a few words, *woman, mamma, Hannah.* I shout at him to let go. Anger surges, white hot. *Suck it up,* my mom had told me once, because I had been crying over a photo I stumbled on in a magazine at the nursing center: Guy with a pretty starlet. *Your dad can't see you like this.* Or when Trudy, in that flimsy, revealing dress, was waiting for us at dinner—I stuffed it down because I had to. No temper tantrums allowed.

"Get up," I tell Donato. "Get up!" But he isn't listening.

I hit him. I hit him again and again—as if the first time hadn't hurt my hand, as if it didn't reverberate through my bones. "You are such a child!" I scream. He is huddled on the ground, trying to shield himself with his arms. My voice is jagged, I am seething. "Grow up," I hiss.

"I will tell them." There are tears on his cheeks, in his eyes. His lip trembles.

I'm astonished by how calm I am. "No, you won't."

He starts crying again, big grating sobs that rack his body. I leave him there, curled on the ground, calling after me, *Mi dispiace, mi dispiace*—I am sorry, I am sorry.

―――

It takes a while to get down the cliff, alone and without help. In the cave Paul and Tonio are admiring the frescoes once more. They stop talking to point out some new detail they've discovered, Paul snapping a picture.

"This is my favorite period of Christianity," Tonio is saying, and Paul nods. "When it was new and rebellious and full of hope."

My cheek stings from where Donato struck me. I'm worried they might see the red spot. *Think of an excuse*, I tell myself. I fell—a stray branch caught me. I could pinch my other cheek and pretend to be flushed. Both of my hands are trembling from hitting him. Had I kicked him too? In my memory I drew blood.

When I come out the other side the sun is blinding. But then, there, spread out on a blanket, are Agostina and Marie eating lunch with Matteo and his dad, who does not look up when I approach.

"Where's Donato?" Marie asks. She's stuffing a roll with *soppressata* and a hard white cheese. There are containers of *taralli* and green apple slices and a bottle of Verdicchio, which is sweating in the sun. "I thought he was with you."

This is when Matteo's dad looks at me.

"He's gone on a walk," I tell them.

Marie clicks her tongue, tickling Matteo. "Boys, no? They are so emotional."

I survey the water for Hannah. When I spot her blond head, I wave and she holds up something for me to see. I shade my eyes, but I can't make it out.

"It's a scallop shell!" she cries. "They're everywhere. Come and see!"

Agostina and Marie are talking in Italian. Nothing about their tone is alarming; it is relaxed, leisurely. But then Matteo's dad glances at me again and the anxiety and fear are nearly suffocating. What will happen? Will Paul ask me to leave? Will Marie press charges—have I done something illegal? It certainly feels that way. I imagine cheap sensational headlines:

AUNT SEDUCES NIECE'S BOYFRIEND
WOMAN, 43, MOLESTS STUDENT, 17

I lack the language to explain the situation. I want Matteo's dad to know that this is not how it was—though that's exactly how it was.

I lick my lips. "I think I'll cool off."

They go on chattering in Italian.

The water is cool and refreshing, and when I reach Hannah I swim past her. I swim and swim until Hannah is shouting after me.

"Aunt Cilla!" She sounds frightened and far away.

I'm tired. I can feel it in my limbs, dense in my chest. All that turquoise, stretching out against the horizon. I replay how Donato covered his head, how he fumbled backward to try to escape me. What must we have looked like on that cliff? An old woman disciplining her child? Two lovers in a heated quarrel? I don't know which is less embarrassing.

I dive and try to reach the bottom. I picture him, not the pathetic Donato tugging at my legs or threatening me, but the Donato in Rome, head tilted coyly, looking at me beneath those curls, raising a cigarette to his lips. Or Guy, how he pushed a loose strand of hair behind my ear before tucking that flower in my dress. But his voice interrupts, cuts right through the memory. *Hush, hush, be quiet. No one can know. The good sister. Ac-ces-si-ble.* It repeats like that. I swim and swim, but the water just returns me to the surface.

"Aunt Cilla," Hannah cries. She looks terrified. Her eyes big and blue, that blond hair, slick and golden.

"I wanted to see how far I could swim." I touch her cheek, which has freckled the way Emily's would during those long summers. "Come on, I'll race you. Last one back is a rotten egg."

She smiles, same smile too. My heart is breaking. "Ready, set, go!"

Hannah tumbles onto the blanket where the others are eating. Paul and Tonio are with them now, laughing and pouring wine into each other's glass. I look around but Donato has not returned to the beach.

I lie out on my towel, watching my niece.

"Papa, I'm fifteen," she says, ringing out her hair. "I've had wine before."

If I close my eyes, it's the same impish laughter. I imagine she's here beside me, lying in the sand. Maybe doing her nails or reading a magazine, humming to herself. I imagine it so well that I don't realize I've fallen asleep until shouting wakes me up.

Hannah and Marie are pointing to the cliff, where Donato has climbed to the highest outcrop.

"What is he doing?"

"He wants to jump, the idiot," Hannah says. "Don't do it!"

"Listen to Hannah, *cuore mio*!" Marie cries. "You will give your poor mamma a heart attack."

Donato must have swam while I slept; his trunks are wet, and his dark hair is tousled from the salt water and wind. I imagine there must be goose bumps on that olive skin. He inches to the edge, peering at the water below. A sudden gust throws him off balance and he reaches for the cliff behind him. Something in my abdomen tightens. This is not what I want. *Get down from there*, I want to yell, but Matteo's dad is standing beside me and I'm worried that something in my voice will betray me.

Agostina is shouting in Italian, trying to persuade him. I can tell by her tone, it's placating and firm—and it almost works,

I see him look at where he must have climbed up. But then Matteo's dad calls out to him.

"Count to three," Donato yells, focusing on the water far below him.

Marie has her hands clasped. "My boy," she says to me. There is fear, but also unmistakable pride.

"*Uno*," Marie and Hannah shout together.

That tightness moves from my stomach to my chest.

"*Due*," they yell.

I think maybe I might faint. *Donato, Donato.* My voice will not work. *Donato, per favore.*

"*Tre!*" they shriek.

He looks up—just a glimpse in my direction, just to see if Cilla is watching. Such a beautiful boyish face—and then he has slipped, his leg catching, sending him headfirst into the rocks below, disappearing into blue-green water.

MONTI, ROME, ITALY

Donato and I are having lunch in a seaside town—one of the whitewashed ones, perched high on a cliff. He is grinning, touching my leg under the table.

Behind him an old woman sits on a balcony. She has a face like a wrinkled pug, and painfully swollen legs, veins bulging green. When she looks at me, I swear it's as if she looks right through me—

But this is wrong. That's not how it was. There was no old woman on a balcony. And Hannah had been with us. The café was in a bustling piazza in Polignano a Mare, with umbrellas angled over our heads, the sun beating down on the slab stone streets and buildings. Everywhere were tourists. Hannah had ordered mussels and complained since eating them of a stomachache. Her forehead perspiring. *Excuse me*, she said, and went to find the bathroom.

There was sudden mayhem in the street. Mopeds and cars were trying to get out of the way of a lumbering hearse, which was driving slowly up the narrow road. It passed so close to us, I could have reached out and touched it.

Death is everywhere, I remember saying once the procession had moved on. And Donato, that smiling youth, was looking at the wine menu. *Does white or red sound good to you?*

Don't you get tired of it? I pressed him. *Living in a place like Rome—or here, which is gorgeous, with its beaches and caves and grottos, but everywhere are reminders.*

He laughed that boyish guffaw. *Los Angeles isn't like that?*

I shook my head, and he got very close—this was when I felt his hand under the table, and that heat in the center of me lapped my insides.

For Italians, he said with that ludicrous grin, *there is only sex and death.*

When I open my eyes, there is no Donato. There is no Puglia. Only the narrow bedroom in Paul and Hannah's apartment in Rome. The writing desk against the wall, the same framed photo of the Ponte Sisto, the turquoise vase on the bedside table, now empty.

I wrap myself in the robe from the *masseria*, which Agostina insisted I keep. It's early, the only light outside is a faint gray smudge on the horizon. When I switch off the A/C unit I can hear a police siren in the distance, trash trucks rumbling down the cobblestone streets. I slide a cigarette out of its packaging. Hannah mentioned where to buy Donato's brand of luxury cigarettes, and I've bought two cases to bring home with me. I climb out the window, onto the slanted roof, and blow the smoke toward the faint moon. Across the way, Donato's window is dark and quiet.

Do not think of Tonio and Matteo's dad splashing out into the water, attempting to swim out to him—or Marie, standing waist-deep in the surf, screaming, *Donatello! Donatello!*

Or later, when I was sitting at the courtyard table with Paul, how I could not explain why I was smoking Donato's cigarettes. Think instead of that lunch in Polignano a Mare.

Will you ask for a dessert menu? And Donato signaled the waiter over, speaking to him in Italian.

That is what I like about you, Cilla, he said, once the waiter left us.

What's that?

He sat back in his chair, stretched his arms behind his head. *You have not tried to learn the language. Hannah was eager to learn. She had to know what was being said. Not you, though. I have to come to you.*

At the time, these moments seemed unimportant—they slipped by like every other second or minute in which seemingly nothing happened. Donato had moved his hand after the waiter returned with our drinks, and Hannah was only gone for ten or so minutes.

Other things I'd forgotten about death: how comforting tea can be when it's overly sweetened with sugar and milk. How beguiling it is that the natural world marches on despite human sadness. The long Puglia afternoons remained the same. Butterflies and wasps flitted about the aloes and palms. Lizards were sunning themselves on the tufa rock. I remember smelling orange blossoms and the Adriatic until we boarded the train for Rome. I think I can still smell it.

There is music coming from Hannah's bedroom. She has stayed up most nights with Marie, going through Donato's things. *You are a great help to her,* Paul had said, kissing his daughter's head. *I'm proud of you.*

My niece comes back with boxes of his stuff. This envelope of clippings from celebrity magazines; this fake gold Timex he bought from a street hustler when he was little. *He saved his allowance and a week later it stopped working,* she told me, laughing but with tears in her eyes. There are T-shirts and sweaters and books.

I want you to take his iPhone, Marie had told her when she came over for dinner last night. *I'm hopeless with these things; see if you can download his music.*

That must be what she's listening to now. It's club music, of course. The bass more prominent than the rest of it. It vibrates the walls softly, rattling the roof tiles.

I'm worried about Tonio, Paul had said to me when Marie arrived alone. I wanted to remind him that death restructures things. He should know that more than anyone. Marie, who cried and wailed, who could not get out of bed—now wants to drink and talk about her son, she wants to look at his photos and hear us say how beautiful he was. But Tonio, who almost came to blows with one of the police who implied that maybe Donato had been high, and then fought with Matteo's dad when he got between them—cannot look any of us in the eye.

Paul must be awake now. I hear his voice, and then the music is turned low.

How can a mother describe her love for her son? Marie had said, as we stood on the balcony, sipping the grappa she brought on ice.

When he was born it was like having the points of the Earth change. It is different from a daughter. I was someone's daughter—but a boy, to give birth to a son, the opposite of yourself—that is a tiny miracle.

I imagine she's right. When I called my mom to tell her what happened, she was distant and upset with me. No matter the tragedy, she was going to hold a grudge. *You should have been here taking care of me*, she complained. She listed weeks' worth of ailments and concerns—and at the end of the phone call I had to promise I'd come home the day after the funeral. *Forward me your flight information so I know when to expect you.*

I rub out the cigarette, tossing the butt into the courtyard below, where the lemon tree is now lemonless. Someone had picked it clean while we were in Puglia. I picture him perfectly—in that moment before he fell, when he was balancing on the cliff—glancing at me, bright-eyed and confident, a smile on his lips, shoulders browning under the sun. Giving me a look that said, *You are wrong, Cilla, I am a man.*

Another thing I'd forgotten: grief can ambush you.

The music coming from my niece's room switches off. I can hear her hiccup-like crying.

I held her while the police questioned us, and made sure she had something hot to drink afterward. I let her wear my pajamas and sleep in my bed with me. She has cried on my lap, my shoulder, and into my neck. If I could ease her pain somehow, maybe it might lessen my guilt.

Yesterday, we spent the afternoon dress shopping for the funeral. I was patient, and obliging, but nothing pleased her. Everything was either too short or too long. She hated patterned dresses, disliked solid colors, would not hear of pants and a blouse or maybe a skirt.

Don't you get it? she bemoaned. *It has to be just right.*

How could I explain that I probably understand her grief better than she does? She eventually gave up and followed me around the women's section of the department store. *But it's got long sleeves*, she said when I came out of the fitting room in a tea-length dress. *Won't you get hot?*

They're three-quarter length, I corrected her, and bought it because I wanted something that would cover every part of me.

I climb in through the window and go downstairs to her room. I hesitate outside her door. Her sobbing sounds almost painful. She is probably surrounded by his things—crying into them. Suddenly the smell of him returns. The feeling of his skin after he got out of the sea, the taste of him in my mouth. I owe her comfort, I know this. But going in there must require something I don't have, because I can't make myself do it.

———

"Ready to go?" Paul says from the living room. He's dressed in a somber gray suit, sitting on the couch where I first saw Donato. A bouquet of peonies rests beside him.

"Almost," I say, fixing studs into my ears. "Hannah's not down yet?"

"She already left for the church," he says, running a hand over his graying stubble. "She wanted to go with Marie and Tonio."

I struggle to hide my relief. "Did she find something to wear? She was agonizing over it yesterday."

"I don't know." He sighs. "She was gone when I woke up, and she wouldn't answer any of my texts. I had to call Marie. Remember how angry she was at Emily's funeral? Christ, it's all too familiar."

"What if we walked?" I need to be moving. I need to feel the muscles in my legs work, hear the heaviness of my step— the simple action of moving one thing from here to there.

Paul looks at his watch. "If we walk quickly. The church is north from here."

It's good to be outside, beneath a cloudy sky. The temperature has dropped, the air more humid than hot. A scooter speeds by, honking as we run across the street. Dried sycamore leaves crunch underfoot.

When we reach the piazza it's packed with people picking

through vegetable and fruit stalls. A vendor presents us a fish fillet as we pass by. I stop to watch a street performer play his violin. He's dressed in a tuxedo as if going to a fancy-dress party. Paul takes my arm, pulling gently.

By the time we reach the Tiber, I've sweated through my dress.

"Are you sure you don't want to take a cab?" Paul asks, and I tell him again, no, no, I'm fine. I catch him glance at his watch. When we cross the Ponte Sisto, I stop to look down at the river. How wide and flat green it is, how timeless it looks. On the other side, a group of teens have taken over the steps surrounding a fountain, laughing and smoking and drinking out of paper bags. It's all hills then, and we hike the cobblestone street in silence except for our panting and the rumble of trucks and cars as they pass us by.

"Let's rest for a moment," I say when we reach the top. "I need to catch my breath."

Paul has removed his jacket, both his cheeks are pink, his forehead glistens. The peonies he's been holding on to look just as sad. "Fine by me," he says, and plops onto a bench. Behind us, Rome stretches out. Pigeons swoop and glide over the duomos near the Capitoline Hill.

"It's nice to be in Rome again," I tell him.

"I keep forgetting you're leaving tomorrow," Paul says, unbuttoning the top button of his shirt. "Hannah is going to miss you."

"I wish I didn't have to go." I look at the nearby apartment building where two children are playing on its stoop. I picture our Malibu house, with its wooden façade, worn from the salty air—the crown molding in each room, the chipped blue-and-white tiles in the kitchen.

Try to hold on to something, I tell myself. The pines rustling in the damp wind, the dog barking in the distance, a man leading a pack of ponies to a nearby park—but it's passing too quickly, and without anything to make it stick. I can almost smell the airport, the jet engines and industrial air-conditioning and food courts. I think I can hear the seat belt click.

"Well, you can always come back," Paul is saying.

"You're staying, then? Hannah mentioned your book with Tonio is on hold, indefinitely."

He shifts his weight on the bench, looks down at his folded hands. "I hope, in time, he'll reconsider. I suppose I could go to London."

"Or California," I offer.

I realize he's trying not to cry. His face is pinched and red. "Did I ever tell you what Hannah said to me after Emily's funeral?"

I can feel the parts of my dress that have partially dried, cold and damp. The two children on the stoop are trying to tempt an alley cat with a piece of cheese. *Micia, micia*, I hear them coo.

"She looked up the stages of decomposition, and she recited them to me. Graphically. She knew about the bacteria and the insects that break the body down." He shakes his head, tears on his cheeks. "How eventually it just collapses, decaying until bones are all that is left."

"Hannah needed closure, she was looking for answers."

"How do you explain death to your child?"

The natural progression of things, the nurse at the rehab center had said. As if it might comfort.

"The ancient Romans believed," Paul says, wiping his eyes with his jacket sleeve, "that if you didn't conduct a proper ceremony and burial, you could be haunted by the deceased. Did we do right by Emily? Did I do right by her? Sometimes I don't think so. Her diagnosis hit me like a thick fog, and I don't think I ever came out of it."

I cover his hand with mine. I want to tell him that I worry about the same thing, but I can't form the right words.

He breathes heavily. "I thought that if I got a hold over it, really studied death, maybe I'd understand grief. But all I know for sure is that you can't hold on to anything. You leave it all behind."

A woman comes out from the apartment and shoos the cat away, taking the children inside.

Paul pushes himself up from the bench. "We'll be late if we don't hurry."

I follow behind, trying not to think of Emily's funeral—how Hannah wore a black dress from Bloomingdale's, her eyeliner thick and dark, a smudge of maroon lipstick—she could have passed for twenty-one instead of almost fourteen. Not a single tear during the service, but then—after everyone had gone home and I was cleaning up plates and tissues and corking wine bottles—I found her looking at baby pictures of Emily. Mascara and eyeliner melting down her sweet little face. I remember I took her down to the beach to try to soothe her. What had I said as we walked in the surf? Those same platitudes, *the natural progression of things*. And I promised to write more. That I would call, that I'd be a part of her life.

By Roman standards, the church is unassuming, but it's grander and older than anything I've seen in Los Angeles. I can smell the incense as we climb the steps, pale colored light falling over the pews from stained-glass windows. "Donato was baptized here," Paul is telling me, but I'm looking for Hannah.

I want to feel her in my arms, smell that thick earthy scent of her hair. Tell her I'm truly sorry.

There is Silvia. I recognize her black hair and green eyes. And beside her, Cristiano, looking choked up, and the two British sisters—but no Hannah.

"Cilla," Marie cries, throwing her arms around me. "You are trembling, *amore*."

Tonio puts his hand on my shoulder, heavy like a weight. "Thank you for coming," he says.

"I understand," Marie is saying. *I understand.* She looks older. There are lines in her forehead, around her mouth. Her eyes are so much like Donato's.

"Like a son," she squeezes my hands. "He was like a son to you."

Several rows away I see Agostina, with Matteo and his dad, and a woman who must be Agostina's daughter. They are talking in hushed, serious tones.

Marie crushes me against her, kissing both my cheeks.

There are other people waiting to offer their condolences, and Paul is steering me away.

"Hannah has saved us seats."

I spot her then, blond and lean and commanding a room even in death. My sister's ghost. She's talking with Marie's girlfriend whose son was best friends with Donato. He's with them too, head down, biting his nails.

"Gabriel," I hear my niece say when we reach them. "You remember my aunt."

I'm ready to shake his hand, to provide a comforting hug if it means I can hurry up and hold my niece, give her the comfort and guidance I should have offered since arriving—but then he flashes a sly grin, eyebrow raised. For a moment I'm sure that Donato has told him everything, but then that look is gone, and he's passive, maybe a bit melancholy, talking to his mother with his finger back in his mouth.

———

I drink the first two gin spritzers quickly. At some point there is a third. The pulsing lights in Club Fluid make the mourners turned partygoers look sped up and slowed down simultaneously. Watching them is nauseating me, I have to look away.

I was ill prepared for the funeral. Never mind that in the last decade I have lost both my father and sister—or that just this year I went to a funeral. One of Mom's old actress friends had died in her sleep. Or a few months ago, Guy called because his dog had escaped and been killed by a truck on Pacific Coast Highway. None of this mattered. When I sat beside Hannah and realized that there, behind the priest, was Donato's body, I began to shake. The same dark curls and plump lips, the same broad shoulders and wide masculine hands, so large for a boy his age. *There he is*, I told myself, but could not keep from feeling that gap, the indescribable space that a person once occupied. Like a black hole, invisible and impossibly infinite.

The music in the club escalates, the dancers jumping along with it. The DJ is shouting in Italian. I catch *Donato* and *danza*—dance, dance, the DJ cries. The crowd is in a furor. Sylvia and Cristiano have closed the club especially for this party. I can see Hannah and her friends, they must know the song. They shout along with it. But where is Donato's best friend, Gabriel?

I thought I felt his small eyes watching me the entire service, and afterward, when we followed the hearse to the cemetery, there he was again. Standing beneath the vault where Donato's casket would rest, watching as Paul and I laid the bouquet of peonies at its base.

You and Donato were close? I tried as we walked to our cars, but he only nodded, pursing his lips a little as he looked me over. And then my niece and Paul appeared, and I had to focus on them.

A pretty girl in a short black dress approaches where I'm sitting with Paul and several of his colleagues from the university. She offers us another cocktail.

"Not for me, *grazie*," Paul says, his colleagues refuse as well. But I need to stay until I can get Gabriel alone.

"I'll have a gin spritzer," I tell the girl.

Paul looks at me surprised. "Don't you have a flight in a few hours?"

"I've already packed, and I don't have to be at the airport until nine." I get up, so he and the others can slide out of the booth. "Besides, one of us should stay with Hannah."

He looks for her on the dance floor. The music has changed, more fluid and deep; the blue lights ripple over the dancers like water.

"At least she's smiling," he says, pointing.

We watch Hannah for a moment, twisting her hips, hands above her head, eyes closed. Not a smear of dark eyeliner, not a smudge of red lipstick is out of place.

She had been stoic during the service. *I want to be with my friends*, she told me when I asked if anything was wrong. The only time she took my hand was after the coffin was fitted into its slot in the cemetery vault, and a worker began to brick up the space. She nearly crushed my fingers.

"I'll make sure she gets home at a decent hour," I tell Paul, but he shakes his head.

"I said she can spend the night with her friends. They should be together right now. It's part of the grieving process."

The pretty girl in the short dress has returned with my cocktail and I gulp it down because everything is happening too soon. The funeral is over, the party is coming to an end. There is Matteo's dad, helping Agostina with her jacket. She waves to Paul and me, Matteo's dad nods. He had stopped to talk to Paul as we filed out of the church. *Mi dispiace*, he said to me, touching my hand lightly. I watch them disappear toward the exit. I've lost track of Marie and Tonio. It must be past midnight; they've probably gone home.

"Good night," Paul is saying, hugging me. "I'm going with you to the airport, so this isn't goodbye."

"That's not necessary," I say against him.

"It's the least I can do," he says, still embracing me. He says other things. About how sorry he is that my trip ended this way, how nice it was to see me, and how he hopes the situation with my mom improves.

I swallow; a good man. At least my sister had a good man.

"Mom has to like one of the nursing homes I picked out, right?"

He nods. The first visit is scheduled for next Monday. A date that is fast approaching—it will come and then march right on through me.

"You're a good daughter," he says, and when he lets go I stumble.

"Maybe go easy on the gin, though." He laughs. "Good night, Cilla."

He squeezes my hand, and then is gone. Absorbed in that mass of revelers, now swathed in red. I realize I've been clenching my jaw for hours. I finish my drink, feeling the alcohol smooth it out.

I watch the crowd of young people—sweaty and pungent and dancing like mad. A strand of hair is stuck to my niece's face. Her eyes are still closed. I shut mine too, just for a moment, just to feel the bass vibrate both of us. When I open them, she is no longer on the dance floor.

I take my glass and push through the crowd. She's not in line for the bathroom, or at the bar, or in any of the booths. I go to the second floor, where it's darker and the music is less frenzied and madcap. Just a few weeks ago Donato and I danced here. The feeling of his hands on my waist, how wonderful my body felt under them.

I search the room but Hannah isn't there either. Although I'm not sure—it's hard to see. I circle the floor, trying to make out the figures on the couches. It's stuffy and smells reminiscent of the rental car after Donato and I had sex in the backseat. I thought Paul or Marie or Tonio—any of them—might recognize that intimate yet universal smell. But none of them did, and the next time we were all in the car, I only had to keep my window rolled down to air it out.

I catch sight of one of the auburn-haired British sisters, disappearing through an unmarked door. At first, I think it's locked, but then the knob gives, and I'm standing in an industrial stairwell, fluorescent and bright.

"Hannah, are you in here?"

The door shuts behind me, and the cacophony from the club—the music, the DJ chanting, the riotous crowd—sounds far away and muffled. I think maybe I hear voices, another door opening and closing. "Hello?" No answer.

The next floor is locked. I can feel the gin now, burning in the pit of my stomach. I keep climbing until I reach the top, where the door gives easily and I'm outside, on the roof overlooking the Villa Borghese Gardens.

"*Zia* Cilla." I hear Silvia's velvety voice. She's sitting with several others, beneath strung-up lights and a cloud of cigarette smoke. I recognize Cristiano, lying on the ground beside her, fussing with a record player, and there is the British sister, leaning over the edge of the building.

"Look at this view!" she says to me. "Can you believe it?"

The moon is big and blue, and hangs over the park, making the trees shimmer in the darkness. The piazza below is quiet, except for the cicadas, and the sound of the fountain at its center, and the occasional raised voice of a cabdriver waiting for a fare. Cristiano gets the record player to work, and jazz spills over and into that silence.

"Not so loud, *amore*," Silvia says to him, and he turns it down to a faint din.

"Is Hannah up here?" I ask.

"Come drink with us," she says, tossing her dark head and patting the seat beside her. "We toast Donato, so you cannot say no."

Gabriel is with them, slouched in a chair, eyes like slits. The moonlight must be playing tricks on me. All of them look illuminated, glossy and lethargic. The only movement is from Cristiano, who I think is kissing the girl next to him. I don't want to stare—but I can hear their mouths on each other.

"Gin spritzer," Silvia says, motioning to my glass. "That was Donato's favorite."

"I know." I immediately regret saying that. I feel heat rise in my face.

"Here, drink," she says, handing me a shot glass. "We toast Donato, *salute!*"

The others stir from their seeming stupor. Cristiano breaks away from the girl. We clink our glasses and down the clear, fiery liquid. I feel it hit my stomach, unpleasantly hot.

"I was looking for Hannah, have you seen her?"

The British sister takes my hands. I feel bad that I can't remember her name.

"She peaked early," she says, touching my face. "You *are* soft. Wow."

I pull away. "What do you mean, *she peaked early?*"

"We're doing MDMA." She smiles, her teeth look fluorescent in this light. "It's okay, we only gave her a half dose. She went to Silvia's with some of the others to go to sleep."

Instantly I remember Emily's later teenage years. She had older friends too, all of them wealthy and reckless. It had started with weekends spent at friends' houses, then spring breaks in the desert. *You should have come with us*, my sister said when she came home looking gaunt and hungover. *It was wild.* What had I said? Only voiced my disapproval. Tried to make her see reason.

"I should be with my niece," I say, getting up. The ground spins, and I reach out for the armchair where Gabriel's sitting.

"Can I talk to you?" I ask him. I motion between us. "In private—alone. You and me." *Talk.*

I can hear that argument between Emily and me. *What's the plan?* I had demanded. *You're going to go from party to party, snorting whatever up your nose? Model for a living? You've turned into Mom.* And Emily, nearly spitting, *If I want your opinion I'll ask for it, okay? Stop mothering me, just stop!*

It wasn't like on the beach, when she laughed at me with those surfers—or later, when we fought about Guy or over how best to care for Dad. It had, at the time, felt like a rejection of me, of everything I had done for her. *Fine*, I remember thinking. *Then I'll wait until you come calling for my help.* I did not reach out, even when she moved across the country. And neither did she. I heard about rehab from our mom. But having a sister is a complex thing. A myriad of major and minor betrayals and confidences, yet some unshakable bond persists. It was why she reached out when she was pregnant, and why I suddenly miss her so much I almost cry out. She would understand, more than anyone, and forgive me.

Gabriel is offering a cigarette. "No," I tell him. "Thank you, no *grazie*."

The sky above us is starless, just matte black and pulsing. "Don't tell Hannah," I'm trying to explain. I kneel beside him. "Hannah can't know." I shake my head. *Never.*

"*Zia* Cilla," Silvia says behind me. "Hannah already knows."

The British girl giggles. "We all know. Hannah found photos on his phone."

It's like jumping from the *faraglione*—not the moment in the air, but when I splashed into the water and felt the weight of my body and the pressure of it exploded in my ears.

"What do you mean?" I ask dumbly.

"And Donato told Gabriel," Cristiano says, and then he switches to Italian. I imagine he's saying something vulgar, because Gabriel snorts and repeats it. My whole face is hot.

"Scandalous!" One of the other girls laughs.

Silvia helps me stand, dusting some grit that has stuck to my dress. She takes my hand and drops a gold chain into my palm.

"Hannah wanted you to have this," she says, folding my fingers over the pendant. I can feel the coolness of the gold, the sharp corners of the lapis.

"And she says goodbye." She kisses both my cheeks. It's a gentle, sweet brushing of her lips. *Arrivederci.*

I stumble inside, down the stairs and into the club, where the house lights are on and the DJ has stopped playing. I can see where the carpet is peeling, the stains on the couches, the waitresses looking tired and worn out. It smells of ammonia and bleach and something on the brink. There it is—that surge again, I'm going to vomit.

In the bathroom I retch into the toilet. My eyes are watering but I don't start crying until I see the necklace on the floor beside me. The gold has been polished, the lapis in the center is deep blue, streaked with flecks of gold. Like stars, like faraway planets. It could hold a whole galaxy within it. I imagine how happy Hannah must have been to have something precious of her mother's. I can picture both of their smiles perfectly.

Light feminine voices come from the other side of the stall door. A polite knocking. They ask in Italian, and then in English.

"Are you okay? Signora?"

Two girls in sequin dresses, purses over their shoulders. Someone's daughters, sisters probably. They help me to the bathroom sink. *Thank you, thank you.* Because one of them is holding my hair so I can drink from the faucet, the other rubbing my back.

"*Passerà*," she repeats. It will pass, it will pass.

I want to tell them about grief, about how after Emily's funeral, when I took Hannah down to the beach, she asked, *Do you miss her?* The surf was so gentle. Kitten waves, Emily would have called them, because they lapped at the shore. *I've been mourning Emily since we were teenagers*, I told Hannah. Because that was what I believed at the time.

"What happened?" one of the girls is asking. She touches the sleeve of my dress. But how can I explain what I have gotten wrong? I did not understand what I had lost.

"My sister," I choke out, tears in my eyes. "My sister is dead."

ACKNOWLEDGMENTS

Second books are strange, feral animals. You need a crack team. Thank you, Daphne Durham, Sean McDonald, Lydia Zoells, Naomi Huffman, Sara Birmingham, Chloe Texier-Rose, Dara Hyde, and Kari Erickson, for being just that.

My love and thanks to Yanina Spizzirri, Gallagher Lawson and Tim Walker, Megan Eccles, Mark Haskell Smith, Linde Lehtinen, and my unwavering source of support, Jordan Bryant. Thank you to my family—I've tried to do right by Papa, may he rest in peace. Thank you also to Karin Lanzoni, Karen Dunbar, and the Michael Asher Foundation for the encouragement. And I will be forever grateful to Tod Goldberg and the entire UCR Palm Desert staff and faculty.

Lastly, this book was written over the course of several trips to Italy, where I'd like to extend my gratitude to the wonderful Rosangela Natalizi Zizzi and everyone at Masseria Brigantino; Alessandra Sperduti in Trastevere, whose Airbnb served as a second home; Marco Proietti, who always welcomed us with a smile; Annamaria Tanzarella and Cynthia Leone at Museo Archeologico di Egnazia for their generosity and time; and Ekaterina Stepanova and Valentina Abodi for their hospitality—thank you, thank you. *Mille grazie.*